# SWEET BITTER REVENGE

# SWEET BITTER REVENGE

Carole St Aubyns

*Sweet Bitter Revenge* published by Rangitawa Publishing
Feilding, New Zealand 2018.



ISBN 978-0-9951046-7-9

www.rangitawapublishing.com
rangitawa@xtra.co.nz

Please note the spelling of Feilding is correct.

**Also by this author**

Sweet Bitter Waters


**Other Rangitawa Romances**

Vote for Love (The Aphrodite Club book 1)
Jemma Daintree.

For all those kind readers who enjoyed Sweet Bitter
Waters.

"In revenge and in love woman is more barbarous than man."
Friedrich Wilhelm Nietzsche 1844-1900


"A woman always has her revenge ready."
Molière 1622 -1673

PROLOGUE

New Zealand Octcober 1895

The post had been left piled untidily on the hall table for a couple of days before she found the time to sort and open the various envelopes hidden between the stacks of farming journals and three newspapers.

One letter caught her eye immediately. An envelope addressed in neat copperplate script to her father. It appeared to have travelled a distance with scuffs and some wear and tear quite obvious. On the back a return address suggested the sender was someone called Keston, West Virginia. Curiosity made her carry the letter into the office where she reached for the thin bladed knife she used as an opener. Slitting through the thick paper she withdrew a folded letter and sat at her desk to read it.

*Chambord House'*
*Allington,*
*West Virginia.*
*Dear Lord Sinclair,*
*I believe you attended Eton school with my father James Keston who died recently.*
*As I intend to travel to New Zealand soon I would like to call on you. On going through my father's papers after his death I think you may have had unfinished business with him.*
*I look forward to meeting you.*
*Yrs*
*Rourke Keston.*

It made no sense to her. The letter was dated January 1895 and it was now nearly October and there had been no sign of the man. Idly she wondered how long it took to travel from America down to the antipodes. Surely not this long so it seemed likely he had changed his mind or been waylaid. Anyway, it made no difference to her in the circumstances.

11

CHAPTER 1

New Zealand November 1895

The gates to the property were imposing, beautifully carved and painted white. They should have been shining in the early summer sun but showed signs of neglect. He halted his horse and read the sign set on the wooden fence next to the entrance. *'Greenleigh'* it stated in large plain lettering. At last, he thought, I'm at the other side of the world and near my journey's end. He was tired and dusty and hoped his host would offer him the hospitality he believed was due to him.

He allowed the horse to walk slowly up the stony driveway that looked more like a farm track than the entry to a large property. Shrubs and trees lined the way and hid what lay ahead until he rounded a shallow bend and saw the house. It was single story and sat perfectly into the gardens surrounding it. A long veranda ran along the front, set with wicker chairs whose faded cushions must have once been colourful. A flight of stone steps led up to a green painted front door with a tarnished brass knocker to greet the visitor. Wisteria wound around the veranda posts with long racemes of pale purple flowers gracefully drooping down and trembling slightly in the tiny breeze. Further along deep pink clematis caught his eye, both climbing shrubs familiar to him from his own garden.

Gladly dismounting from the livery stable horse, he stretched to ease his stiff body and wound the reins around a metal ring set in a post near the steps.

He pulled his jacket straight, took a deep breath to help compose himself, before he climbed the steps and raised the knocker.

## CHAPTER 2

She loved Sundays. It gave her a respite when her small staff went off to church in Feilding and she had the run of the house for a few hours of absolute privacy. Today she'd decided to clean the library something that had long been overlooked as unimportant in the daily life of the farm. Dressed in a sacking apron, her hair covered with a scarf, she set to with plenty of good intentions until the dust gave her a terrible attack of sneezing. It was only as she was finally drawing a normal breath and finished blowing her nose that she heard the sharp rapping on the front door and a voice calling through the letter box.

'Coming,' she answered hurrying out into the hallway.

She wiped her hands on the apron and walked towards the front door. It took her a moment or two to wrestle with the stiff bolts which had probably not been opened for some months. She finally pulled the door open to greet the visitor who turned out to be a tall figure with his back to her.

'Yes, can I help you?' she asked as he heard the creak of the rarely used door hinges and spun round to face her.

'My name is Keston. I've come to see Lord Sinclair.  Wrote to him earlier on this the year.'

Although his introduction was terse, he had a pleasant deep voice with an unusual accent. He held out a visiting card taken from his pocket and she took it between two rather grubby fingers. As she read it, she realised this must be the mystery man who had written the letter from West Virginia. He wore a wide brimmed hat which shadowed his face but she was aware of white teeth and almost black eyes under dark frowning brows, peering at her keenly.  Her hesitation must have been obvious because he moved a step closer and she knew he had to be examining her scruffy appearance which immediately made her nervous and her red nose started to tickle again. Completely by mistake she pulled out the duster from her apron pocket and blew her nose on it before she realised her error and hastily held it behind her.

'What's your name?' he asked abruptly and it occurred to her he must believe her to be a servant. She found that quite amusing and decided to deceive him until he revealed more about his purpose. Over the years she learned to be very cautious when approached by strange men especially good looking ones like him.

'Merryweather sir, my name is Merryweather.'

'Well Miss Merryweather, I've come a great distance so please may I come in while you fetch your master?'

Merry took an instant dislike to his patronising tone and the way his eyes ran over her body. She promptly made a mental note never to address her servants, such as they were, in such a manner. She pulled the door open wider and gave a small parody of a curtsey and watched as he strode into the hall as if he owned it. It was at this point she had a sudden sense of her world shifting but she mentally shook her head as she walked past him and opened the door to the drawing room.

'Please wait in here,' she pointed and shut the door quickly after him not offering him a seat or refreshments.

She picked up her skirts and ran down several corridors until she reached her bedroom where she tore the scarf from her hair, smoothed a few stray tendrils back from her face, threw the apron on the floor and grabbed a flannel to wipe the dust from her face and hands. A quick look in the mirror told her she was reasonably tidy in her plain grey dress and she walked calmly back to the stranger waiting for her although, inwardly she felt a growing sense of trepidation. What had her father done to bring this man here? Was there to be another revelation about his life that would make hers even harder than it already was? She took a deep breath before she went back into the drawing room. Surely she had uncovered all her father's secrets by now?

## CHAPTER 3

Rourke inspected the room carefully. It was tidy and smelt of beeswax and lavender but the furniture was past its best and the sofa cushions were faded. The room did not feel lived in and there were few ornaments or pictures to give it character or a sense of family usage. There were no photographs above the fireplace and no clues about who might inhabit this place. Even though it was a warm and sunny room there was an air of bleakness about it, a lonesomeness. How ridiculous, he thought, how can a room possibly be lonely? And yet there was an utter stillness in this room as if it was waiting for life to begin again, as if the people who had once laughed here would return and give it a meaningful purpose once more.

He walked over and stood at the window, pulling back the lace curtain to check on his horse tethered to the post in the front garden. When he heard the door open quietly, he took his time to turn and acknowledge whoever had entered behind him. After all he did not imagine he would be greeted with any great friendliness in this house. But he had promised his father to carry out his bidding and it was too late now to retreat. When he saw Merryweather again, he sighed impatiently.

'Is Lord Sinclair not at home?'

Merry mentally gritted her teeth but she smiled sweetly at her visitor as she gestured to a large arm chair set by the fireplace.

'Mr Keston, won't you sit down? Would you like

a drink perhaps? You must have had a hot ride here today. I presume you've come from Feilding?'

'Just fetch him will you?' he said rudely as he lowered his tall frame into the chair with some reluctance. 'And yes I'll have a scotch please.'

'Very well,' she said and went to the sideboard where a decanter and crystal glasses stood on a slightly tarnished silver tray. It was the last of the cellar that her father had laid down and there would be no more. With his hat and gloves removed she could see her visitors' dark hair curling over his collar and his hands were quite rough as his fingers touched hers when he accepted the drink she held out to him. She watched as he took a large swallow of the amber liquid as if his life depended on it. His eyes widened in surprise as she sat on the sofa opposite to him with her hands folded demurely in her lap. Damn he thought, there's something going on here I don't understand. This woman had an air of possession about her that didn't speak of service. She was beautiful for a start with large grey eyes under finely shaped brows. Her face was expressive and intelligent with soft pink lips that were pinched together at the moment. Had he made a mistake? Was he at the wrong place? Why did he get the feeling that the room had begun to come to life when she smiled at him?

'I'm sorry to tell you that Lord Sinclair died over a year ago. You may have had a wasted journey.'

Her voice was soft but held no emotion. Her words had made him sit back in his chair they were so evidently unexpected.

'Oh….' He digested this news with obvious

difficulty and she noticed his fists clenching as he leaned forward after a moment of reflection, frowning at her. 'So are you the housekeeper here? Are there new owners?'

Once again her smile lit up her face but he sensed it was polite and not particularly friendly.

'I'm Merryweather Sinclair his daughter, although I'll forgive you for thinking otherwise. I'm not dressed for visitors today as you can see. I was cleaning the library.' She stopped herself from mentioning that her staff were absent in case it put her at a disadvantage.

His mouth dropped open and she knew instinctively he was having difficulty digesting this news, and she had been correct in him judging her to be a servant. Nevertheless, as he placed his empty glass on a small table beside him, he did not immediately own up to that misunderstanding. He sat up straighter, obviously gathering his thoughts. She waited patiently to hear what he would say next. It was a trick she had employed on a regular basis with her father when he was at his most difficult and raving at the world. It was easier to become a hard silent wall he hurled insults at than to argue with him. It conserved her energy for all the important tasks his illness had thrust upon her shoulders. Eventually this stranger would tell her why he was here, she was sure of it so she bided her time until he decided to reveal his purpose. He was an extraordinarily attractive man and it was no hardship on her part to let her eyes roam over his face and his hard lean muscled body. She gave her imagination free rein about his attributes and how she might benefit by them if the chance ever arose! Dreams were all she was allowed these days. Eventually her patience was rewarded as he spoke in his soft drawl.

'My apologies ma'am. I'm sorry I mistook your position here. Please accept my sincere condolences on the loss of your father.'

He sounded sincere but there was still an edge of arrogance about his words as if he begrudged her position; her power in her own home.

'Accepted,' said Merry. 'But truth be told we are all much happier without him! He became a very bitter man after my mother died. Nothing I did was ever going to please him especially when his drinking got worse. I find being my own mistress here is much easier.'

Her down to earth cynical statement made Rourke Keston feel as if he was in danger of completely losing control of the conversation and the situation he now found himself in. This was not going to the careful plan he'd decided on all those months ago when he'd sorted through all the documents in his father's safe. His promise to his father made with all the sincerity of an obedient son, now appeared to be far more difficult to achieve but he came back to reality as he heard her speak again.

'So please tell me why you wished to meet him? You sound American. Is that correct?'

'Yes, from West Virginia. Our fathers were friends at school....'

'Oh yes,' she interrupted him. 'That's right, you sent a letter recently. I remember now thinking how long it took to arrive here. I did read it but I never actually thought you'd come all this way just to dig up past history with my father.'

He nodded, acknowledging she was correct.

'It did take me some time to travel here because I own a tobacco farm and the harvest went on longer than anticipated. I'm on my way to the South Island, somewhere called Nelson. I've been told the climate is suitable for tobacco down there and I'm looking at the option to buy land and plant it.'

'So there's no opportunity for you to expand your holding at home?' Merry asked and he was struck by her astuteness. It was unusual for the women he knew to take an interest in his work and her sharp intuitive comment sparked awareness in him that was perhaps a warning of her acuity.

'No. I already own everything that's suitable for miles around.'

It sounded to her as if his statement was made from the absolute confidence he had in his wealth and ability. Merry had met other men who had this self possession and she had not liked them but she was perhaps being a little harsh. Those other men eyed her up as an asset they might acquire not as an equal in any way. There was no such impression from this man. She remained silent wondering what she was supposed to say to Mr Keston who had arrived so unexpectedly. It was hardly his fault her father had died and was not present to greet him and reminisce. In fact it would have been an embarrassment when she recalled what Lord Sinclair had degenerated into. She was allowed to be thankful for that at least.

The American reached for his glass again before

he noticed it was empty. Merry pointedly ignored this and did not offer to re-fill it. He looked up at her with his dark stormy eyes set in a face that appeared to be brooding on something she could only guess at. His clothes gave him the look of a foreigner. The black, fine wool jacket was long, in a style not usually seen locally, and his tie a mere ribbon formed into a neat bow. His trousers were tighter than most of the  men  she  knew and  fitted  his  long  legs to perfection right down to his boots which appeared to be made of some sort of dark lizard skin with a low heel. Merry couldn't help thinking that he just needed spurs to be the complete cowboy she recalled reading about somewhere in an article about Wild Bill Hickock. She decided it might be better to move the conversation on, to take her mind off this man's physical attributes which  she found overly attractive despite his owning a blunt temperament. She smiled at him and swore there was a reaction in those calculating eyes of his. Well she would try that again!

'Perhaps there's something I can help you with or had you just wanted to talk to my father about your father?'

'This is very difficult for me,' he said shifting in his seat and then sighing. 'I'm afraid you probably won't like what I have to tell you. Nevertheless I have to say it because I made a promise to my father to sort out his affairs. After he died I went through his papers and found this.'

He pulled out a leather wallet from inside his jacket and extracted a small slip of paper. He looked at it for a moment and then passed it to Merry. She unfolded the note and read the contents. Her face betrayed nothing which surprised him. As she handed it back to him she said, 'This is an IOU for £10,000 signed by my father. What does it mean?'

'It means that your father owed mine £10,000 which he borrowed, possibly to buy this farm, before he came to New Zealand and my father went to West Virginia. They were both living in London at the time. My father was generous to a fault and subsidised many of his friends. His father sent him to America to make him mend his ways but my father being the charmer he was fell on his feet, met my heiress mother and married her. Luckily he couldn't distribute her dowry because her father had been warned and put it all into trusts and investments. That curbed any spending sprees my father might have set out on. But getting back to our business, as far as I can work out, this debt has never been repaid and I'm here to collect it. Before my father passed away he asked me to tidy up his affairs so that my mother was not inconvenienced in any way.'

Merry wondered why she would be worried about some far off woman being *inconvenienced* when she had a son like this to look after her. Did he not realize how *inconvenient* it would be for her to repay him or possibly lose her property? She took another more careful look at the IOU he held, which was stained and creased. She wondered if it had been written out in some London gambling hell. From what she knew of her father it was extremely likely.

'I can see your father's name isn't mentioned and there's no date. My father's dead so surely that makes it invalid? I can't make out why you would expect this to be still legally valid after all these years?

Would it stand up in a court of law I wonder?'

Still quite calm he noted, as she eyed him coldly. Strangely it pleased him, this stoic attitude of hers. He had never had time for histrionics by women.

'I don't agree. When Lord Sinclair made his purchase of this land, he sent the deeds of the farm to my father as security against the loan. At that time he must have felt he could repay it. I took the time to go back through all my father's bank records and ledgers to ensure I hadn't missed a payment but I'm afraid there was nothing recorded.'

Rourke Keston pulled an envelope from his inside pocket and handed it to Merry who gave a deep resigned sigh and pulled out the contents. She opened out the folded document and looked over it with a puzzled frown.

'These must be a later copy because they show the house site drawn in,' she said. 'I have the original deed which only shows bare land so I don't know if yours have any validity, even so you must be aware that I'll need time to check that my father didn't pay that loan back. This has come as a complete surprise to me and I have to ask you why you've decided to call this debt in?'

'Sure you have the right to know that. As I said before I promised my father to make sure his will and last wishes were carried out and to do that I have to gather in any debts owing to him. This is the last one and probably the most difficult. It's certainly the largest. I wish to buy land in South Island and this money will help me do that. I'm afraid that if you can't pay me, I've taken legal advice which said I'll have the right to force you to sell this property to recoup the money.'

'Which action, you need to know, would make me homeless and without any income,' said Merry softly but with a distinct edge of steel in her voice. 'But you don't appear to have any sort of conscience about that. What sort of man travels halfway across the world to deprive a woman of her living and her home? I presume your mother didn't lose her home when your father died? She didn't suffer that *inconvenience?*'

Again Keston shifted uncomfortably in his chair, the stress in her words affecting him as he looked around the room trying to find the right explanation. The last thing he wished to do was to be involved in any sort of moral argument with her. He knew she might win. He had always prided himself on being an honourable man but his loyalty lay with his family not with Miss Sinclair, this seemingly implacable woman.

'You seem to be reasonably well off Miss Sinclair. This is a large property of over three thousand acres if those deeds are correct. You must make a very good living from the farm. I'm quite sure you will pay this IOU but if you don't, believe me I will insist you sell the property. I made a promise to my father before he died that everyone who owed him money would be asked to repay it. He was somewhat foolish in his younger days and overgenerous to his friends. Our family suffered the consequences of that for years.' A blatant lie but he felt it was valid. 'I'm afraid I'm not made in his mould and I believe debts should be repaid however long they've existed and however it affects those who have benefited by his largess.'

He watched as she sat back in the chair, her eyes narrowed and calculating when she looked at him. The news that her home could be sold over her head appeared not to worry her unless she was a very good actress. He had not told her the whole truth but why would he concern himself with that? She had no right to know of his present circumstances. All the same her assertion about losing her home was chilling and not something he had anticipated. Anyone giving a superficial look at this property would assume she had adequate funds to pay him or could raise them. If that was untrue then he was about to be the worst rogue she had ever encountered and it did not sit easily with him. He cursed both their father's for putting him in this position but he had made a vow and he never broke his word. What really worried him was her disdain for her father. Would she be able to dismiss his debts as nothing to do with her? He swore inwardly. He should have checked on the legal situation here in New Zealand about this matter as well as the opinion he had sought in America. He resolved to find a lawyer in Feilding tomorrow and ask a few pertinent questions without revealing who was the subject.

'Mmm…' she said and then she smiled at him graciously as if dismissing his claim preferring to move onto more important sociable matters. 'I'm really being a terrible host. Would you like another drink or perhaps a cup of tea?'

He shook his head and replaced the documents back inside his jacket. 'No thank you,' he murmured trying to ignore the feeling in his chest that something had happened here which gave her the upper hand.

But despite his misgivings about coming here he was still determined to remain staunch in his dealings with this matter. Nothing would be gained by being swayed by a pair of dreamy grey eyes or a mouth so fascinatingly soft he ached to touch it. Instead he focused on her determined chin and her ability to side step his concerns with ladylike coolness. It must be his travel weariness affecting him this way, there was no other explanation. His taste in any permanent feminine company, leaned towards the blonde, petite and submissive young ladies who were the local occupants of the West Virginian marriage market. Other than that he took his pleasure with more earthy women who made few demands as long as they were paid. When, at some far future date, he chose to wed, he would wish his new wife to be compliant and decorative not assertive and confident in her own skin like Miss Sinclair. Not for the first time since he had entered her home, he admitted privately he might have come up against a worthy opponent.

'Well then,' she said still smiling sweetly. 'I'll obviously need to confer with my lawyer and my bank manager. I trust you'll give me a reasonable amount of time to sort this out. Do you have proof of your identity because as far as I'm concerned you could be anyone? After all there have been no witnesses to our conversation today and I'm not completely ingenuous.'

'Of course,' he said taken aback that she would even doubt him but then he recollected he was a stranger and a foreign one at that so perhaps she was well within her rights to be suspicious. 'I'm happy to provide anything required to your lawyer and I intend to stay in Feilding for about three weeks. Is that long enough?'

'Who knows?' she responded with a vague wave of her hand. 'I've never had to do anything like this before so I can't tell you. I do think it will be up to you to prove the debt is genuine and still owing. You will appreciate I am not going to capitulate until I've explored every avenue available to me. Where are you staying?'

'At the Feilding hotel. You can reach me there when you've found out anything or made your decision.'

'I'll let you know in a few days as to how I'm progressing then,' she offered pleasantly. 'Perhaps you'd like to return another day and ride round the farm with me to give you an idea of what is involved in a sheep farm in New Zealand. You grow plants and I grow grass. There must be some similarities I'm sure. You'll quickly exhaust the pleasures available in Feilding so perhaps I could send you a note when a time suits me?'

Once again he was bemused by her placid outlook. It appeared she was prepared to treat him with all the politeness of a welcome guest who she had to entertain and amuse. Should he be suspicious of her he wondered? But then again she was a woman on her own and probably more vulnerable than her father. He'd expected to stir up anger and remorse when he entered this house instead he'd met with civility and he found it difficult to deal with. There was something about this woman which unsettled him. He had also read New Zealand women were renowned for their political freedom and he supposed she was used to making her own decisions now that her father was dead. It was noticeable she wore no rings and made no mention of a husband in their conversation. He mentally crossed his fingers hoping she would not prove difficult and place obstacles in his way. He could not allow himself any sympathy towards her. By all accounts her father had been a rogue who had reneged on his debt and it was now time to collect. If his daughter was made of the same stuff he would have to tread carefully to ensure she did not find a way to cheat him. Rourke had learned the hard way not to place his trust in anyone, unlike his father whose good nature and soft heart had left his son to sort out the ramifications of his generosity.

Merry stood, smoothed her skirt down and left the room, as he followed her. She wrestled with the front door and refused his help as it creaked open. Stepping out into the bright sunshine he put his broad brimmed hat back on and held his hand out but she ignored it.

'I don't usually shake hands with the Devil Mr Keston,' she said. 'Best if we keep this businesslike I think. I wish you good day,' and she turned and went back into the house closing the front door firmly behind her.

Rourke took a deep breath and ran down the steps to his horse. He didn't look back as he rode down the driveway but he felt a shiver of unease as he passed through the front gate out onto the road. A premonition passed through his mind that all was not going to be easy with the lady. She had been far too collected for his liking and he wondered when he would hear from her again. In fact he looked forward to it. She might prove a worthy adversary if he could keep himself from being distracted by her charm.

When she opened the door to him on his arrival, he had been so tempted to gently wipe the smudge of dust from her cheek as her long lashed grey eyes regarded him with such clear suspicion. Do not even think about her as a woman he told himself. Just treat her as a debtor who owes you a large amount of money. He would allow her no sympathy and no amount of pleading would change his mind. He never changed his mind!

Closing the front door Merry leaned back against it, almost panic stricken by the sudden threat that Rourke Keston believed he held over her. She cursed her wretched father for putting her in this position. It was untenable to think anyone could believe all her hard work over the past years could be destroyed overnight. Even though she knew there was no way the American could gain anything by taking the farm away from her, it would involve a great deal of trouble. She wondered how she could deal with the situation to her advantage and a smile lit her face. He was after all a most attractive man, to be honest, the most handsome man to come her way in years. Not since Jack had she felt such a strong attraction to a male but then her smile disappeared as sadness engulfed her.

Bother, come on Merry, she encouraged herself, this is your opportunity to enjoy yourself for a while. Mr Keston has no idea what he's let himself in for and with that thought boosting her confidence she returned to her dusting. Determination and doggedness had kept her sane these past ten years. She had good friends to advise her and her commitment to the farm and ability to run the property successfully could never be questioned. The tobacco grower from West Virginia would discover the sheep farmer from New Zealand was well able to fend for herself in more ways than one!

## *CHAPTER 4*

The next day found Merry riding her grey mare Starlight the three miles along the road to Totara Hills, the property of her friends the Wyndham's. Like Merry, Jane Wyndham was a farmer and before marrying her husband Gareth, had come to New Zealand with her young son and established her property on her own. There was little Jane Wyndham did not know about farming and Merry had come to rely on her sound advice. Jane and Gareth had been married for nearly seven years now and had a six-year-old daughter. Recently Gareth had successfully stood for Parliament. He was an excellent politician who took great trouble to listen to the trials and tribulations of his electorate and Merry knew this couple would give her good advice regarding the way to treat Rourke Keston's claims.

Trotting up the driveway to the house through plantations of eucalyptus trees, rhododendrons and camellias, Mary guided her horse around to the stables where a very efficient stable lad came running out to meet her. She thanked him as he took Starlight away for a drink and made her way up to the back veranda and into the kitchen where Bessie the cook was kneading dough on the kitchen table.

'Miss Merry!' She exclaimed her face full of pleasure. 'It's good to see you. Jane's in the library and Susie is just about to take morning tea into her. Add an extra cup Susie and announce Miss Merry please.'

The maid smiled and led Merry up the hallway into the library.

"Miss Merryweather is here to see you ma'am,' she said formally and placed the tray of tea things on a low table by the fireplace.

Jane Wyndham was busy entering figures into a large ledger as her friend arrived and she stood up and came out from behind her desk and greeted Merry with a hug and a huge grin. Since her marriage, Jane had blossomed and on her husband's insistence wore stylish and colourful gowns unlike the plain attire of her former single life. These accentuated her slender figure and smooth shoulders and showed off the beautiful aquamarine and gold necklace she wore today. Such a contrast to the practical gowns she had hidden behind as a supposed widow. Today she wore a light green silk skirt that almost floated around her and a white muslin blouse with elbow length sleeves edged with lace. For a moment Merry thought wistfully of the single strand of pearls her mother had left her but pushed her envy deep down.

'Oh it's lovely to see you. Now I have a good excuse to stop working and gossip. Do sit down and tell me why you're here,' she said as they settled themselves in the two leather wing backed chairs on either side of the fireplace, which at this time of the year held a dried flower arrangement.

As Jane busied herself pouring their tea, Merry looked around the room. There were book cases filled with a vast collection of volumes from Jane's grandfather's house in England which she'd inherited and piles of farming magazines stacked everywhere.

As she took a cup of tea, Merry eased back in the seat and sighed with pleasure at being in this lovely room. Jane was her closest friend and she was certain to have a good idea about how to deal with Rourke Keston. She also knew a great deal about the intimate life of Merry Sinclair and how her past had shaped the staunch personality of this attractive young woman.

'I had a visitor yesterday. An American from West Virgina called Rourke Keston turned up and said his father and mine were at Eton together.'

'Don't tell me he came all this way just to meet your father.'

'No he didn't. Well he did expect to but really he came to tell me my father owed his £10,000 and if I can't pay him he'll insist I sell  my farm!'

'What! Are you serious?' Jane put a cup and saucer down on the table and leaned forward with an incredulous expression on her face. 'How could he possibly believe that?'

'He produced an IOU in my father's handwriting. It was for £10,000, but I noticed it never mentioned his father's name so I don't believe it can be valid. However he also had a copy of the deeds for Greenleigh which he said my father sent as proof he'd spent the money on buying the property. I only looked at them quickly but they appeared to be a copy made later after my father built the house. I know that the original deeds don't show the house site.'

'What does he expect you to do? Hand over the money or the farm without a fight? Is there any way you can prove that your father paid the debt back?'

'I don't know to be quite honest. I could look

back through his ledgers but it would take me such a long time and he wasn't very good at bookwork at the best of times. I've been keeping the books for the last nine years ever since I was sixteen, so it certainly didn't happen during that time. If it was before I doubt he made a record of it. Father was incredibly vague about financial matters when it suited him and especially after Mother died and he started drinking. Anyway I told Keston that it was up to him to prove the debt hadn't been repaid. I was so taken aback that was all I could think to tell him.'

'Quite right,' said Jane thoughtfully. 'Gareth is out today meeting people in his electorate but as soon as he gets back I'll tell him about this. He may have a better idea about how to deal with Mr Keston. I must say he sounds very hardhearted man.'

'Yes, you're right about that. I should have laughed in his face knowing the true story but some demon inside me wants to see him eat his words. I've decided to spin this out as long as possible. I should keep him on tenterhooks until he comes to me begging for a decision.'

'Well at least you're on safe ground as far as the farm is concerned,' said Jane. 'But I hope he hasn't got some other threat he can produce. What did he seem like?'

A wicked grin crossed Merry's face as she finished drinking her tea and put the cup and saucer down. Jane leaned forward as she saw the gleam in her friend's eyes.

'Well...' She answered. 'He's a most attractive man, probably the most handsome one I've met since

Jack. That's going to be to my advantage. I have a feeling he won't be above falling for a few seduction techniques. I rather fancy having some pleasure dealing with Mr Keston.'

Jane roared with laughter.

'You minx!'

'Well there are no likely prospects for a husband around here but that doesn't mean I have to be a dried up old spinster does it Jane? I'm a modern woman and I see no reason why I should be deprived of physical love if I choose to go out and find it without a wedding ring.'

'And what if he turns you down?' Jane's question hung in the air and it was a few moments before Merry could think of an answer. 'Well I'll just have to deal with that when it happens I suppose,' she smiled wryly. 'However Jack and I learned a great deal about intimacy, growing up together and I dare say I can take Mr Keston by surprise. I could do with the challenge Jane because as I'm sure you understand, all work and no play can make one a very dull person!'

'Oh I agree,' nodded Jane. 'My life changed completely when Gareth came to work here. I hadn't realised what I was missing! Seven years later I'm still making up for it which is absolutely wonderful. In fact sometimes I have to admit I simply can't get enough of him. Life without physical affection does tend to narrow one's outlook.

'Exactly my point,' agreed Merry. 'Although looking at Mr Keston I imagine numerous women have been falling over him for years. I do hope he's not married,' she added as an afterthought.

'Essential that you find that out very quickly my dear,' said Jane. 'Just don't give your heart if he succumbs to your charms.'

'I don't think I could ever give my heart to a man who can so cold bloodedly expect a woman to hand over her property like he does. He should be more concerned about his heart which is obviously frozen solid.'

'I can't wait to meet him,' Jane responded. 'What say we have a party and invite him? It will be a good excuse to use our new ball room. Dinner, cards and some dancing might soften him up nicely. Just a small do about fifty or so. Would you like that?'

'I would if I had a suitable dress to wear. You know how I tend to live in my oldest clothes out on the farm.'

'Oh, don't worry about that. I have several rather beautiful gowns that Gareth has bought me over the years and I've never had the opportunity to wear them. There's one particular dress with a neck line rather too low for me to wear. My darling husband bought it before he knew about the scar on my breast. Every time we go to Wellington I mean to take it back to my dressmaker to alter but I've never got around to it so it seems like serendipity you need a frock and I have just the thing. Come on, no time like the present, let's go upstairs and have a look. You shall go to the ball Cinderella!

In Jane's dressing room Merry was astonished at the array of gowns hats and shoes that were on display. She stood looking around her in amazement. This was such a contrast to her own meagre wardrobe and something inside her felt a twinge of envy even though she would never be able to afford to outfit herself in such sumptuous materials. There was also the obvious fact that as a single woman well on the shelf according to society, she was not invited out anywhere much where she could wear such beautiful outfits. She watched as Jane went through the dresses until she found what she was looking for.

'Here we are. It won't be quite long enough because you're at least an inch or two taller than me but I think we can remedy that with a temporary lace frill around the hem.'

Merry gasped at the beautiful gown that Jane displayed to her. The fabric was a deep iridescent green and the bodice was boned and covered with fragile black lace. To wear such a dress would be every young woman's dream and Merry was no exception.

'It's quite wonderful,' she whispered, reaching out to run her hand over the crisp silk of the skirt. 'I've never owned anything like this.'

Jane reached for the bell to call her maid Emma.

'Emma will help you into it and she'll sew something around the hem to make it the right length. She's wonderful at dressmaking.'

Unfastening the buttons of her plain blouse and removing her skirt, Merry stood quietly waiting for the fitting in her well washed and darned petticoat and thin chemise as Emma arrived.

'Oh Miss Merryweather, ' she clapped her hands together as Jane explained how the gown needed to be lengthened. 'Here let me help you into the gown.'

'You'll have to take off your chemise,' said Jane.

'The neckline is too low and it will show. There's no room for modesty wearing this frock! We want you to show yourself off not cover up!'

Rather embarrassed, Merry allowed Emma to pull the chemise over her head and stood naked to the waist and Jane grinned as she looked at her friend.

'Where have you been hiding those spectacular breasts my girl? Talk about hiding your light under a bushel!'

Merry blushed and the two other women laughed. Between them they lifted the gown over her head and smoothed it down over her hips. Emma fastened the tiny fabric covered buttons at the back of the bodice and pulled the neck line straight.

'Look in the mirror,' requested Jane. 'You look like a completely different woman. Who would have guessed?'

Her reflection caught Merry by surprise. Who was this elegant creature with a tiny waist and creamy breasts that threatened to spill out of the low lacy neck line which was supported by two slender straps over her shoulders. Yes she decided, this gown is made for seduction and I shall use it to my advantage if the chance arises. Would Rourke Keston find her desirable dressed like this? Or would he still view her as the woman with dust on her face and a plain serviceable frock that she had owned for years? Only time and the opportunity would tell.

'I have some shoes that match,' suggested Jane. 'Can you find them please Emma? If you can wear those we'll have a better idea about the length of the skirt.'

'I can't thank you enough,' said Merry. 'I never dreamed I could look like this.'

'Oh you'll look even better when I've done your hair,' said Emma. 'Can you lend her a necklace ma'am?'

'Yes of course. I'm sure I have something suitable. These emeralds perhaps.'

Emma produced a tape measure and went off to the sewing room to find some suitable lace to add to the hem of the gown. Jane undid the buttons and helped Merry to remove the garment.

'Best if you get dressed here on the night, I think. Then I can be absolutely sure you're a picture of perfection! Mr Keston will be astonished at your beauty. I can guarantee it.'

'I hope so,' laughed her friend. 'That bodice fits extremely tightly. I'm not sure if I'll be able to breathe much while I'm wearing it but I have heard that one must suffer to be beautiful!'

'Apparently so but I'm afraid I tend to lean towards comfort most of the time,' offered Jane. 'Breathing is so essential I find!'

Dressed in her ordinary clothes Merry gave one last longing look at the gown before accompanying her friend back downstairs. As they walked through the kitchen Jane said to Bessie, 'We've been planning a party Bessie. I'll let you know when we've decided on the date and how many people are coming.'

As the two women walked back to the stables Jane remarked, 'When Gareth returns I'll ask him to go into Feilding this week and see if he can arrange to meet Mr Keston and make it look quite casual. It's better if the invitation comes from him rather than you then he won't suspect anything.'

'What a good idea,' agreed Merry. 'It mustn't appear as if the evening has been set up for the purpose of us to be together again. That's the last thing I want him to find out.'

Two days later Merry received a note from Jane advising her that the party was to be held in a few days on a Saturday night. Jane had arranged that before then her husband Gareth would come across Mr Keston at the Feilding hotel and introduce himself as the local politician and issue an invitation. All the arrangements were proceeding smoothly so far.

CHAPTER 5

Merry spent some time the next day, searching for any financial records that her father may have kept from his time in England but with no success. She even poked her head up into the attic but it was empty of any clues. Lord Sinclair had never discussed his childhood with her and as far as she knew there were no living relations back in England. The dusty old ledgers kept in the library revealed no proof that he had ever paid back the £10,000 to Keston's father. On an impulse she harnessed up Starlight to the dog cart and went into Feilding to visit the bank manager. He met her request with some surprise but agreed to ask a clerk to look back in the bank archives to check if such a payment had ever been made but after a protracted wait, it appeared there were no records to show this.

On her way out of the bank she walked into a tall, solid figure. Squinting against the sunlight she peered up at him as he grasped her arms to steady her. For a brief moment she stood still, held close to him, breathing in his scent of cigar smoke and warmth before she stepped back in haste when she recognised him. He seemed reluctant to let her go but slowly removed his hands.

'Miss Sinclair, I'm so glad we've met,' he said. 'I was wondering if you'd taken the chance to talk to your solicitor yet. Time is moving and I would really like to get this all sorted out as soon as possible.'

'Oh! Mr Keston,' Merry said, stepping even further back from him in a hurry. 'I'm so sorry I didn't see you with the sun in my eyes. No I'm afraid my solicitor is away in Wellington for a week. I'll certainly let you know when he returns and I'm able to talk to him. Like you I'm eager to seek a solution to your problem.'

As she spoke she smiled sweetly up at him while crossing the fingers of one hand behind her back hoping against hope he would not ask who her solicitor was. The last thing she wanted was for Keston to call on him only to find the man was still in Feilding and she was procrastinating to stall for time.

'That's most unfortunate,' he said pinching his lips together. 'But it can't be helped I suppose.'

It occurred to Merry that perhaps she should give him some information just to keep him happy.

'However I have just been to visit the bank manager,' she offered gesturing to the building behind her. 'I'm afraid he couldn't find any record of my father repaying the debt. I've also started to search through my father's records at home but so far with no luck. That's all the news I can give you at the present I'm sorry to say, on behalf of both of us.'

She offered him a wan smile this time, hoping it made her appear eager to please him when quite the opposite was the case. He looked away from her up the main street and sighed. Merry could swear he was gritting his teeth and she supposed he was finding it very inconvenient to wait around for some sort of action from her. His next words proved her point.

'To tell the truth I'm becoming extremely bored of this town. I think I've visited all the pubs and the library at least twice.' He graced her with his lazy grin.

Merry seized this chance offered to her, to renew her invitation. She daringly leaned a little closer to him and placed her hand on his arm as if she was about to deliver a confidence to a trusted friend. As she looked up at him she saw a spark of amusement and perhaps affection on his face but it was fleeting.

'In that case please accept my invitation to come out to the farm and I'll take you for a ride around the property. We could have a picnic lunch by the river. That might make a change for you and fill in some time. You could come tomorrow if you are free. Around ten o'clock?'

He gazed down at her and once again she was caught by those brooding eyes of his and felt a slight tremor go down her spine. What was it about this man that caused her to feel so discomfited? She hoped he could not read her thoughts and gave him a brighter smile to encourage him to accept her offer. My word she was certainly extending her ability to show friendliness in a variety of facial expressions! She hoped the effort was going to be worth it!

'Thank you. I would really like that,' he said and gave her such a mischievous grin she nearly took a step backwards as her face reddened under his scrutiny. So he did possess some charm which gave her great hope in her plans for possible seduction should it prove necessary. Perhaps she need not wait until the party to start softening his attitude towards her? She would ask her cook to pack the picnic lunch tomorrow and she silently prayed for good weather. Mr Rourke Keston would find he had bitten off a great deal more than he could chew when he decided to commandeer the

the rightful property of Miss Merryweather Sinclair!

## CHAPTER 6

Rourke was surprised at the repeat invitation from Merry. He wondered what her motives were because certainly she didn't want to spend time with him because she liked him. He was under no illusions about her estimation of his character. He had been forced into the situation by a father  who in his youth, had been just as much a spendthrift  as Lord Sinclair but there was no way he was going to explain this to Miss Merryweather. Indeed it seemed that both their fathers had put them in this untenable position by some strange juxtaposition of fate. That she had offered the hand of friendship made it all the more difficult for him to treat her as an adversary or a means to his own ends. To be honest it had never occurred to him that he might be in the position to make someone he was coming to respect, homeless and it didn't sit well with his conscience.

His friends back in West Virginia would be laughing fit to bust themselves at the situation he found himself in. They had wagered on his success and now he was mighty glad he hadn't entered into the betting. It was up to him to make the best he could of the position he found himself in but even after only two meetings with the lady he was becoming increasingly unsure he could carry through the threats he made to her.

Every time she looked at him with those beautiful wide grey eyes he saw storm clouds and he imagined there could be thunder and lightning hidden under her calm exterior. Still he'd always felt drawn to women with passion and fire in their blood and he judged Merry Sinclair to be a worthy opponent. Who knew there might be a great deal of enjoyment ahead of him in the next few days that he'd not anticipated? So far his heart had never been captured by any particular woman and it wasn't about to be lost now so he felt quite safe in that respect. Bachelorhood suited him. After all how could he travel like this if he was hampered by a wife and perhaps children? It was inconceivable that he would ever give up his single status for the sake of a pretty smile and a pair of grey eyes. However, he wasn't too high and mighty to refuse a woman if she offered herself.

He liked women, liked their scent, liked them in his bed; never left them unsatisfied or unhappy when he moved on. Something in him wanted to provoke Merry Sinclair, wanted to crack that cool exterior and he would welcome the chance to set fire to her temper and her desire. A large part of him wished he had met her under different circumstances, that the promise his father had imposed on him could be forgotten or laughed off so that he could have approached her as a man admiring a lovely woman and nothing more.

## CHAPTER 7

As he rode up the track to the stables at Greenleigh the next day, Rourke Keston looked around him with interest. They were tidy and clean but there appeared to be only one stable boy who came out to greet him as his hostess led her mare Starlight out into the bright sunlight of the yard.

'Good morning,' he said tipping his hat slightly. 'We're lucky with the weather.'

'Yes my prayers must've been answered last night,' she smiled and he noticed she was wearing a divided skirt. A loose man's shirt tucked firmly into her waistband opened at the neck and her outfit was topped off with a wide brimmed hat like his own. Her hair hung down her back in a thick braid and Rourke felt a twinge of jealousy as the stable boy cupped his hands and gave her a leg up and she sat astride and urged her horse over to his side.

'Are you ready?' she asked. 'We won't rush. I'm not sure how much stamina your livery horse has but we better not push him too hard. The hills are quite steep at the back of the farm.'

'No I think you're right,' he conceded. 'There wasn't much choice really and it was hardly worth my while to buy a horse for such a short stay.'

He followed behind her as she urged Starlight along the track behind the house. He could not help himself from looking at her trim behind sitting so well on the saddle. Used to riding in a western style, Rourke has let his stirrup leathers right down so that his legs were almost straight which felt much more comfortable than the English style of riding used in New Zealand and he was glad he had the foresight to pack a pair of long riding boots. They ambled up a valley where a large flock of sheep hardly moved as the pair rode by. There was a smell of sweet grass and the greasy tang of sheep's wool in the air. When they reached the crest of the first hill Merry brought Starlight to a halt and turned to him. She pointed back the way they had come and for a moment Rourke felt disorientated as he looked up at the sun expecting this to be the south they were facing instead of the opposite direction. He must get used to being south of the equator now and the sun rising in the northern sky.

'I always like this view. I feel like a bird looking down on the house and over to the mountains.'

'I see what you mean. Is that mountain snow-covered all year round?'

He squinted against the bright light and pulled the brim of his hat lower. Merry grinned at him knowingly as if she knew her next comment would shock him.

'That sir, is a very active volcano. It's called Ruapehu and round the back, just to the north, there's one called Ngarahoe.'

'Good heavens! Are they dangerous? How far away are they? The near one looks so close today almost as if it was floating on the horizon.'

'Eighty miles as the crow flies I believe. You're right it does look closer but they haven't erupted for quite a while and usually the smoke and the ash doesn't reach this far.'

'Well this is a first for me. I've never seen a volcano before although I have to say this is as close as I wish to be!'

Her companion grinned at her and she noticed how well he sat on his horse. He rode in a manner that was completely foreign to her, legs stretched out, reins held in one hand while the other rested on his thigh. His hat was tipped down over his eyes which were narrowed against the sun and he held a small cheroot clamped in his mouth even he spoke. Then, as if he read her thoughts that it was rude to speak with his mouth full, he pulled it out, pinched the end off and stuck it in his pocket. Merry tried to keep her eyes off those long legs and the muscular thighs with which he controlled his horse so well. Ah well, she thought, if all goes to plan I wouldn't mind seeing a lot more of them and she fought to keep a grin off her face. She turned Starlight and continued up the track which led to further higher hills behind them and called out over her shoulder.

'When we get higher you'll be able to see another volcano over to the west. It's called Mount Egmont and it's very beautiful, much more conical in shape; not so rugged as those to the north.'

Once again Keston was almost mesmerised by her graceful form as she urged Starlight ahead of him. It was not hard to imagine her as a warrior queen leading her men into battle. She seemed unfazed by the fact that many people would consider it inappropriate for her a single woman to be out alone riding with him and no chaperone. All at once he was very pleased that society appeared to be so much freer in New Zealand than back in West Virginia where indignant mothers would have been pursuing him and accusing him of taking advantage of their daughters in the same situation. All things taken into account he was having a very good time here today and his determination increased as he wondered how he could take advantage of her attitude.

They stopped several times in their travels over the farm so that Merry could explain to him her farming practices and how they might differ from the ranches in America. Rourke appreciated her clear commentary on different grasses in the pasture, the way she had left groups of native trees still standing to allow shelter for the animals from the prevailing westerly wind and the way their drinking water was siphoned around from huge ponds or dams, as she called them, to fill the many drinking troughs in the paddocks. Her competence came through clearly as she spoke and her visitor found his interest held as he watched her face express her love and passion for her farm and her animals. It was not often he encountered such vivacity and enthusiasm in a woman and it suddenly began to mean a great deal to him to achieve her friendship no matter what the result of his quest turned out to be. It was extraordinary she felt able to confide her attachment for the land to him even though he represented a threat to everything she held so dear.

'I could leave the dams unfenced,' she explained. 'But the sheep gets so muddy trampling round the edges to get a drink and that affects the wool and stains it so I prefer the troughs. They have to be cleaned out occasionally because they get full of mud and frogs but that is balanced by the better price I get for my fleeces. And it's not much fun trying to pull sheep out of the mud when they get stuck or cast.'

'Much more practical,' he agreed. 'I can see you give a great deal of thought to the humane treatment of your stock and that must always pay off in the end.'

'That's until some new disease crops its head up though,' she said ruefully. 'We go through gallons of cider vinegar which we dose the sheep with. It's pretty good at killing the internal parasites but there are other problems that aren't so easily treated I'm afraid. Weather conditions change so quickly here and the grass can hide all sorts of nasty things that will attack the sheep externally. But on a better note it won't be long now before we put the rams out and I really enjoy lambing. I never get tired of seeing how strong they are even in the worst conditions.'

'Perhaps they are a little bit like you  Miss Sinclair,' Keston said without thinking and she had the grace to blush which only sent an inexplicable shiver of arousal through her guest which surprised him.

'Not at all like me Mr Keston. They have to brave the wind and rain whilst I can go inside, have a hot bath and sit in front of the fire. Possibly the orphan lambs are the lucky ones because I bring them into the kitchen and stick them in front of the stove.'

Her companion braced his thighs tightly against his saddle in an effort to control his errant body and his horse shifted under the pressure. Rourke searched for the polite response to her observation and fought to concentrate on her words instead of her soft pink cheeks which begged to be caressed and kissed.

'What I meant is you appear to be a very resourceful woman. Obviously your circumstances have forced that on you in some ways but you seem to be very practical in the way you run the farm.' He considered her words for a moment. 'Possibly tobacco farming is a lot easier and certainly our climate is more reliable but we also are subject to very nasty diseases and pests that can ruin the crop overnight.'

She seemed to accept his compliment and very soon they were riding down towards a wide stream where she dismounted and led Starlight down to the water for a drink. Rourke followed her example and admired the crystal clear water tumbling over the rocks forming small deep pools where he was certain he could spot trout. When the horses had their fill, they let them graze nearby and Merry removed the leather bag and the blanket which had been stowed behind her saddle. She walked towards a patch of grass set among a patch of bracken under a tree and removing her leather gloves, unrolled the blanket and spread it over the ground before she sat down and opened the bag.

'I'm afraid it's only bread and cheese,' she said. 'And a few apples. I tend to live very frugally these days but I expect it will hold off your starvation for a while.'

She carved off a slice of bread from a home-made loaf and folded it around a piece of cheese before she handed it to him with a napkin. He reached over and took the food in both hands feeling the warmth of her skin brushing his and noticing how her hands were quite rough and reddened with blunt short nails. Not for the first time he wondered why a woman like her indulged in physical labour. Was it purely for love of this place or was there another reason? Should he ask her? But then again it was probably not the most diplomatic thing to ask a woman on such a short acquaintance.

'It's been many years since I've eaten outside,' he admitted. 'But we used to picnic a great deal when I was a boy and my mother was still alive. There's a spot on my farm very similar to this and sometimes she even allowed us to go skinny dipping.'

'Be my guest,' was his companion's most unexpected response and he looked up at her in surprise. But she showed no reaction and continued to munch on her bread. Rourke took a bite of his bread to prevent him from taking her up on this. It would be astonishing to see her reaction if he was to strip and dive into the river. The very thought of it made him shiver but it was not from the anticipation of the cold water. It was from the hope she might follow his example! There was no chance of this he decided as she watched him calmly and he knew she was testing him.

'Thank you for the offer but I don't think it's appropriate for me to take you up on it.' Then he added with that sweet smile of his, 'Perhaps another time?'

His grin became more mischievous and Merry felt her cheeks grow pink once more and turned away, wishing she had not been quite so blatant. She would have to learn to be more subtle with this man but the thought of him stripping his clothes off and diving into one of those deep pools made her feel heated. It would not do to appear too eager at this stage. Today was just the first foray into the plan she intended to follow. A mere dipping of toes into forbidden currents perhaps?

'Perhaps...?' She paused. 'To be honest I would love to take my boots off and have a paddle but it's so hard to get the sand off my feet afterwards and there's nothing worse than putting gritty toes back into your shoes.'

Keston took a long drink of the lemonade she poured for him and inwardly he sighed at her practical response but what else could he have expected from her.

'Children have so much freedom, don't they? As we grow older we seem to put so many barriers around enjoying ourselves but I suppose that's what keeps us all on the straight and narrow path. Well most of us,' he surmised.

'I do sometimes come here to swim when it's very hot,' Merry admitted. 'It's the most marvellous feeling even if it's freezing cold. It was one of the few skills my father taught me that was some use. When I was about ten I had this fantasy that a dragon lived in the cave just around the bend there.' She pointed over to the cliff on the other side of the river. 'One day I swam down there and peered inside.'

'And there be dragons?' offered Keston.

'No but a pile of gigantic bones. It was quite a shock. As if a dragon had been there and this was his leavings from all the prey he'd devoured. However when my father came to look he said they were Moa bones.'

'Moa...?' he queried.

'Yes. They were a gigantic bird that inhabited

early New Zealand. They were quite common and taller than an ostrich. Unfortunately they were also very tasty and early inhabitants hunted them out of existence. But their bones are often discovered.'

Keston tilted his head and gazed at her and she could sense a question evolving in his mind. She readied herself to rebuff any probing in to her father's character. The past was the past and having Keston here was enough reminder of events she'd pushed far back in to her memory and had no desire to recall. But she discovered it was an entirely different subject that intrigued him.

'Can I ask the origin of your name? I've never met a woman called Merryweather before. It sounds more like a surname, not a girl's name.'

'Blame it on my father's perverted sense of humour, ' she said. 'I was born during a bout of awful weather. Rain, hail and roaring gales, apparently. The roads were so badly flooded, the Doctor couldn't get here from Feilding to attend my poor mother. To add insult to injury I wasn't the son and heir my father required so he called me Merryweather. Quite cynically so.'

'The opposite of bad weather then?

'Good Lord no!' she laughed. 'Merryweather, because he was tipsy and under the weather!'

Rourke shouted with laughter at this unexpected explanation and knew he must reciprocate with a story of his own.

'My mother wanted to call me Storm because like you I was born in a particularly nasty bout of weather but Father wouldn't allow it.'

'Storm would suit you,' Merry commented. 'You do have a brooding look in your eyes sometimes and you have a kind of growly voice.'

Once again she had an uncanny knack of seeing into his character which unsettled him.

'My mother always said it's not the thunder you should be afraid of, it's the lightning,' he whispered thinking of his earlier assessment of her, as she stretched both arms above her head and leaned back against the trunk tree behind her. It was a languid natural gesture but the movement caused the neck line of her shirt to open wider and Keston caught his breath at the sight of the pale skin and the slight swell of breast. Unconsciously he shifted closer to her and reached out with a finger to touch a button that was hanging loose against her bare neck.

'You've nearly lost that button,' he said his voice quite hoarse as his finger brushed her skin.

Merry looked down and gently removed his hand before she caught the loose strand of cotton, pulled it tight and wound it around the button before pushing it back into its buttonhole. 'More mending,' she sighed. 'Just another thing to fill up my idle moments. That is of course when I'm not busy crocheting doilies and painting mediocre landscapes. Such are the respectable pastimes of us spinsters.'

Keston sat back and his gaze was warm.

'I can't imagine you do any of those? This place must keep you very busy. You have many staff… a farm manager?'

'That would be me,' she replied with a shrug. 'I have a cook, a maid of all work, the stable lad and two shepherds.'

'That doesn't sound very many to run a place this size.'

This revelation could also explain her careworn hands he realised.

'I manage and there's a shearing gang locally who travel around all the farms in the district so I hire them for the main wool clip and other animal maintenance.'

'You have time for any sort of social life? It seems a pretty bleak existence for a young woman.' He hesitated and added, 'I mean I do understand how all the crochet and painting must be so fulfilling but even so…?'

A mischievous smile lit her face this time and she gave him a very knowing look. A look that shot straight to his loins, and caused him to turn away from her slightly, before she noticed the state of his interest manifesting itself in his trousers.

'It can be a little dull especially in the winter evenings, so one has to make the most of any opportunity that comes along. Don't you agree? But of course there are dances and…interesting visitors.'

Without warning she leaned forward and ran her finger lightly across his bottom lip and he grabbed her wrist and held it to his mouth saying,' Are you trying to seduce me Miss Sinclair?'

'Do you want me to?' She whispered leaving her hand in his. *Yes, yes* he nearly whispered but decided caution would repay him better. Her skin tasted sweet against his lips and he was tempted to pull her close but he was wary of his situation. The sun was nearly overhead and he felt a trickle of sweat down his back. Honesty had always been his policy however trite that sounded at this moment

'I'm always ready to pleasure a beautiful woman but I wouldn't want you to think you can change my mind by flirting with me.'

'I think that goes without saying but there's nothing wrong in two consenting adults enjoying themselves is there? A little afternoon delight?'

Merry gazed at him and ran her tongue over her bottom lip quite unconscious of the effect it would have on him.

The sun shining through the leaves threw patterns over her body as she rested back against the tree. The sharp clicking of cicadas filled the air and dragonflies flitted close to the river. In the distance the far cry of a sheep only added to the drowsy atmosphere. Keston weighed up the risks of getting too far involved with this woman then ignored them as his body became even more heated and his eyes roamed over her soft mouth. He slid close to her taking her face in his hands as his lips gently moved over hers before she put her arms around his neck and gently licked his mouth. With a groan his tongue explored the inner softness she opened to him and he felt her breasts pressing against his chest. She tasted of cheese and lemonade and suddenly it was the most sensuous flavour he had ever encountered.

The realisation came to him that this woman had enjoyed passion and pleasure with a man before and he vaguely wondered what had happened to that lover. Merryweather Sinclair set his blood on fire and he reached down and slid his hand inside the neckline of her shirt. To his astonishment he discovered she was wearing nothing underneath the rough cotton and he cupped her full breast in his palm circling her nipple with his thumb until it was hard and she squirmed against him. Lifting his head he sat back slightly and un-fastened her buttons pushing the shirt down over her shoulders and looking down at her nakedness. He bent and took a breast in his mouth teasing and tugging until she moaned and pushed him away.

'You'd better take your shirt off now,' she commanded gazing him through narrowed eyes that were filled with desire. He sat watching her for so long, his eyes full of dark intent until she wondered if he'd changed his mind so she sat up and decisively undid the buttons opening his shirt and ran her hands over his chest. Keston could not believe the sensations she aroused in him and sat bemused. Merry felt the warmth of his skin and gazed at his broad chest, admiring his muscular shoulders and his flat hard stomach. It was so hard to resist reaching for the large silver buckle of his leather belt to release the long, thick shaft pressing against his trousers but she refrained.

Rourke grunted, swallowed hard to dampen down his desire and pulled her into his arms, her head resting against his chest and its' covering of fine dark hairs. Her hands explored his chest, her thumbs teasing at his nipples, stoking fires in him that must be quenched. He held her tightly until his breathing slowed and he managed to come to his senses.

'I think we both need to calm down,' he whispered against her hair. 'No good can come of this as much as I would like to play the rake and ravish you.'

He was trembling under her cheek, his heart beating fast and his hands reaching under her shirt, soothing her bare back belied his words. For a brief moment she recalled Jack and his tender love making but this afternoon she had wanted to be taken roughly, swiftly and mindlessly by this stranger. There would have been no sentiment in their coupling only pure lust but she was mistaken in her assumption he would agree to satisfy her wishes. Why did she think this man would erase her harsh memories of the past when everyone and everything else had failed? She pulled away from him with an audible sigh that tore at his heart.

'I'm sorry,' she said. 'Please forgive me.'

His gaze was quizzical but he sensed her withdrawal was not to be questioned and he gently pulled her shirt together taking one last longing look at her body as she fastened the buttons with fingers that shook slightly. This moment would be stored in his memory for ever when he left here — the picture of her among the ferns her beautiful shoulders bare above the white shirt she clutched around her to cover herself.

'It's for the best I think,' he smiled. 'You know nothing about me. Why would you risk your reputation and your body with a man like me?'

'What sort of man are you?' she asked her head down. She could not bear to look at him. If only she could stop him seeing her remorse. She began to wish she could turn back time, this afternoon and retract her wanton behaviour.

'The sort who gets his own way usually,' he warned and his eyes were cold as he buttoned up his shirt. 'You should be more careful when you invite strange men to ride with you. They might not all be able to resist you.'

In answer she reached into the pocket of her divided skirt and pulled out a small handgun which she placed demurely on her lap. Keston drew back in shock and she finally found the courage to look at him.

'Come now Mr Keston, don't look so surprised when you come from a country where we hear everyone carries a pistol. Don't take me for some green girl. That would be a big mistake. I never go anywhere without this. Mainly because often I have to dispatch a sick sheep and I'm not too good at cutting their throats. A bullet is much more humane wouldn't you agree? Although if you want me to I can show you the gutting knife I keep on my saddle.'

Her guest swallowed hard and nodded. Merry's voice had lost its softness and become businesslike again.

'I guess you're right there. It *is* better to be kind to animals. Just don't use your weapons on me please. I have every intention of being honourable, I can assure you. But I'm sure you understand that where I come from, if you point a gun at anyone, you mean to kill them.'

'That's a moot point,' stated Merry. 'Anyway I've never even winged anyone and I think we have different definitions of honour sir.'

She put the gun back into her pocket and ignoring his frozen stance, packed up the remains of their lunch and stood and waited until Keston shook the rug out and rolled it up again and they fetched the horses and continued their ride.

## CHAPTER 8

Rourke was preoccupied with the assured way she had handled the gun and also with the picture of a naked Miss Sinclair splashing around in the river on her own. He became increasingly uncomfortable as the thought aroused his cock again, which made riding somewhat unpleasant for a little while. He finally noticed that they were trudging up a long hill facing south and was surprised to see a small graveyard fenced off with white wooden palings. Merry stopped in front of it and gestured to the two gravestones standing facing to the south. When she spoke her voice was calm and gave no hints of what had transpired between them at the picnic.

'My parents are buried here. They both loved this view. We're looking directly south, down towards Wellington and you can see the Tasman Ocean today on your right, and those dark shadows on the horizon are the South Island. In fact we're probably looking almost straight down to Nelson and the area you wish to farm. You're lucky it's so clear today. I remember coming up here as a small child and seeing the Southern Lights. It was spectacular. I'd never understood how relatively close we are to Antarctica until then.'

It was hard to believe this woman was the same person who had sought seduction such a short while ago down at the river. Her transformation into an informative tour guide was instantaneous and he missed the warmth of their earlier companionship.

Her visitor took a deep breath of the warm air and looked where she directed. To his left bush covered ranges as far as the eye could see going south dividing the island in two, and ahead the ocean, a thin blue line on the horizon. Nearer he could see a dark island rising from the sea with sharp peaks.

'That's Kapiti island,' supplied Merry. 'It was once the home of a famous Maori chief and if you turn to your right you might just be able to see Mount Egmont the other volcano I promised you.'

He followed the direction she was pointing in and found what he thought was a cloud on the horizon was actually a beautifully symmetrical volcano covered in snow. It looked tiny from this distance but she assured him it was every bit as big as Ruapehu and looked down over the city of New Plymouth.

'I don't think I'd like to live there with that hovering over me. I feel much safer here,' he stated. 'We certainly don't have such dramatic scenery where I come from or such threatening natural features. It's a much softer landscape.'

'Wait till you experience an earthquake, ' Merry grinned.

'Ah! I have, so you can't surprise me with that. I stopped in San Francisco for a few days before taking ship here and the ground shook one night.'

'Mm…' pondered Merry her face serious. 'You're certain it was an earthquake and not some opera singer?'

Keston regarded her with a glint in his eyes and she felt her stomach react under his scrutiny. 'Do you always try to provoke your guests so deliberately Miss

Sinclair? Or is it just me you're intent on sharpening your claws on?'

'I'm sure I don't know what you mean,' she replied. 'But let's face it you haven't exactly come here to endear yourself to me have you?'

'And I'm sure you do understand perfectly,' he responded ignoring her other comment, and then as if it were an afterthought, 'It might have been both now I think of it!'

This induced a gasp from Merry who looked across to him as her horse sidled restlessly. He gave her such a wickedly sinful smile that for a few brief moments she felt a jolt of potent jealousy because of the woman who enjoyed him on that night; in fact, about all of the women who had ever been bedded by him. Shaking her head she yanked rather heavily on Starlight's reins and headed back towards the farmhouse looking back over her shoulder to ensure he was following her.

Neither of them spoke on the ride back. Hanging between them was that sweet episode by the river. Merry was already beginning to regret her forward behavior and Rourke was questioning why he had been so sidetracked by this beautiful girl. He vowed not to let anything else get in the way of his purpose even if he found her almost irresistible. There would be no more dalliance between him and Merry Sinclair if he was to be able to achieve his father's request. He must remain oblivious to the woman who stood in his way. But in spite of all these noble thoughts he couldn't take his eyes off her back as they went swiftly along the farm tracks towards the homestead.

How he wished she was a plain homely woman who treated him with deference. Hell and damnation, she should have been frightened of him but instead she had almost ignored the claim he made and treated him like a welcome visitor.

When they reached the house she dismounted and looked up at him.

'I'll bid you good afternoon Mr Keston. I'll let you know as soon as I hear from my solicitor.'

And without another word she handed the reins to the stable boy and disappeared inside the house. Rourke watched her go puzzled by the change in her mood but he shook his head and made his way down the driveway out on the road. Best to get back to his hotel and dinner and maybe find a card game amongst the other guests. It was quite clear he was going to have to wait around before any further progress was made. He fervently hoped it would not be too long or the strain of resisting this woman was going to severely test his mental and physical strength.

## CHAPTER 9

'What you mean you took him for a tour around the farm?' asked a puzzled Jane Wyndham the next day. 'I would have thought the less you saw of him the better.'

'Of course you're right, you always are,' muttered Merry. 'But I thought he might understand my position a little better if he saw what was involved and how hard I have to work on the land. I was wrong of course but I suppose we had a pleasant day. There seemed no harm in asking him at the time and he was quite charming. It was nice to have some company for a change. I don't get many chances to talk about my dreams for the place. Perhaps it made him think about what it means to me?'

She gave a small smile remembering how good he felt under her hands and the sinfulness of his grin that transformed his face from stormy to sunlit.

'Did you pull your gun on him?'

Jane had come to know this young woman very well over the past few years and was never surprised at how well she could protect herself. She also knew that Merry couldn't resist shocking people sometimes.

'Well…'

'I knew it,' laughed her friend. 'You'll really upset him if you go on like that. There must be much nicer ways of finding out about him I'm sure.'

'Mmm… Well I tried that too,' Merry admitted. 'I thought it was going quite well then he suddenly retreated and put a great deal of distance between us. I suppose it wasn't the best idea in the circumstances but he is rather delicious and I rather forgot why he's here. I guess I'm just a trollop at heart when a handsome man comes within reach of me. That's what my father always said and let's face it I didn't prove him wrong.'

'Well perhaps you've learned another hard lesson in that case but of course you're not some loose woman Merry. Your father was a bastard by all accounts and you must never let his opinion of you shape your life. He was a bitter old man when he sent Jack away and he never improved. Not many daughters would have looked after him as well and as kindly as you did. But to get back to Keston, it's all very well to have some fun but you must remember he wants to deprive you of everything that you've worked so hard for even if he doesn't know it's impossible.'

'I shall go and have another long talk to the bank manager tomorrow. I have to know if my father did pay back that money or not. Much as I wish to make this stretch out long as possible it's probably better to get it sorted and rid myself of the worry.'

'I whole heartedly agree with that sentiment,' nodded Jane. 'Then you'll be free to have your fun with him! At least for a short while.'

'How wicked of you to even contemplate that of me. I don't really want a dark tempestuous man in my life but a little passion wouldn't go amiss. Anyway it's all supposition because I'm probably not his type at all even if I do fling myself at him again.'

'Well you can't go on holding a candle for Jack for the rest of your life so if the opportunity comes to enjoy a handsome sensual man I think you should grab the chance before he disappears.'

'Like you grabbed Gareth?'

'Absolutely,' laughed Jane. 'And look how well that turned out.'

'No regrets then?'

'Oh my God no! He's heavenly as far as I'm concerned and I just wish my foolish pride had let me tell him so a lot sooner than I did.'

CHAPTER 10

The next day Merry harnessed the dog cart and once again made her way into Feilding. It was Friday and the town was full of farmers come to participate in the stock sale. As she drove past the Sale yards she could hear the bellowing of cattle, the bleating of lambs and smell the strong ammonia odour of penned animals. She wondered if the Wyndham's were in town today and waved out to several other people she knew.

On reaching Kimbolton Road, she got down from her cart and tied up Starlight to the hitching rail before she entered the bank. After waiting for a few moments she was ushered in the manager's office. Mr Brownlie was a large man rather self-important but nevertheless he treated his clients fairly. Merry was indebted to his sound advice and knew he would give her a fair hearing.

'Now Miss Sinclair what can I do for you today? Brownlie said making sure she was seated comfortably in front of his large desk. 'If I recall correctly this is your second visit the bank this week? Is something the matter? Did my clerk not deal with your query? '

'I'm afraid not,' smiled Merry. 'I did talk to your clerk on the earlier occasion but he wasn't able to help me.  It requires further investigation I think only you can assist me with.'

'Well tell me all about it,' he said and folded his hands on the desk.

'As you know shortly before my father died he

mortgaged the farm to pay back all his gambling debts that had accrued over the years. I suppose at the time he thought it was the best thing to do. When he became ill he seemed to have a fit of conscience but while I agreed about his fine gesture, I had no say in this. He gave no thought to how it would affect my future. You will know that I have done the very best I can to continue repaying the bank but when I looked at the figures your clerk showed me it occurred to me my father may have borrowed extra money and I wondered if there was any way you could tell me if that was the case and who he paid it to?'

'Your father was very deeply in debt in New Zealand but let me call my clerk to bring in the file then we might be able to clear this up.'

'There is one particularly large debt that was owed to someone overseas and now their son has arrived to claim it and I can find no records in my father's ledgers to prove that he repaid it. I'm wondering now if he took it out of that mortgage money in which case you may have a record of that payment here at the bank.' Mr Brownlie called the clerk and requested the file on Greenleigh farm. When it arrived Merry was horrified to see how thick it was but the bank manager reassured her that the bulk of these papers were simply copies of bank statements.

He shuffled through and eventually found documents pertaining to the mortgage her father had raised about two years previously. 'Let's see,' he said. 'It appears your father wrote out checks for most of these debts and they've all been cross-referenced to the bank statements as they were cleared but there was a second mortgage of £10,000 that was sent out of New Zealand by bank draft. It was never shown on his bank statement, an obvious oversight of ours by the looks of things I'm afraid. However I note it was added to the first loan so you have been repaying it.'

'That's the sum I'm looking for,' said Merry excited by this discovery which could vindicate her treatment of Keston. 'It went to America didn't it? To a Mr Keston in West Virginia?'

The bank manager looked puzzled for a moment and then fixed her with a slightly embarrassed expression on his face. He coughed and read the document again before placing it back on his desk and clearing his throat nervously once more.

'I'm afraid not. According to this statement the money was sent to lawyers in the south of England, in Brighton to be precise. The instruction to them from your father was that it was to be paid into an account belonging to a Mrs Finlay.'

'I've never heard of her.'

Merry sat back in her chair, suddenly filled with apprehension. Was this a mistress that her father had left behind when he came to New Zealand? Was she a relative Merry had never heard of? There appeared to be no explanation and certainly no connection to Keston's father in this payment.

'I could send a telegraph to these lawyers requesting information about the lady if you would like? Is it her son who has come to claim this money? If so, he's trying to trick you because it has obviously already been paid. A few months before Lord Sinclair's death according to our records.'

'No I don't think he's her son. His name is Rourke Keston.' Merry tried to gather her thoughts. 'He says he's the son of a man who went to school with my father, at Eton.  According to him, his father lent mine the money to come to New Zealand, buy our farm and build the homestead.

'As far as I know his mother Mrs Keston, is still alive. His father married her when he went to West Virginia. She's an American and as you just said this payment was only made to the lady in England just over eighteen months ago.'

'Well I can go ahead if you wish and make enquiries about this mysterious Mrs Finlay but in the meantime I suggest you ask Mr Keston if he knows anything about her. It appears very suspicious to me. Please let me know what you want me to do.'

'Yes I suppose it does and I suppose I must,' admitted Merry. 'But it's not going to be easy.'

Mr Brownlie nodded but offered no further insights as he stood and shook her hand.  She made her way out of the bank unhitched Starlight, climbed into the dog cart and slowly made her way home. She would have to invite Rourke Keston back to the farm and try and discover what he knew about this mystery woman in Brighton.

## CHAPTER 11

Rourke sat in the hotel bar gazing into his whisky trying to work out why Miss Merry Sinclair persisted in haunting his thoughts. He scowled when he remembered how soft she felt in his arms yesterday by the river. None of these recollections helped him to keep his purpose strong in his mind. The promise he made his father on his deathbed had to be kept but it was becoming increasingly hard to believe that his demands could be obeyed. It was clearly evident, even in this very short time he had known Merry that she did not have access to the money he was demanding and he doubted if he would have the sheer cold heartedness to take her farm in payment. He had never ruined anyone let alone a single woman who obviously worked her heart out to keep her inheritance solvent. In fact the more he thought about her the more he wished her well, admired her and yes, dammit wanted to take her to bed.

But where was the point in that? A brief satisfaction of desire perhaps? Deep down he was afraid it would not be enough to indulge his appetite for her, to taste her and bring her to completion under him. He dare not become enamoured with the lady. It was all far too complicated to even contemplate.

These lustful thoughts were interrupted by a tall distinguished man he had never seen before, coming up to his table and speaking to him.

'Mr Keston?'

'Yes,' said Rourke surprised.

'I'm Gareth Wyndham local member of Parliament. I heard you were in town visiting Miss Sinclair. I'm afraid news travels fast here especially via the bank manager. She's a neighbour of ours so I decided to track you down and introduce myself. I hope you don't mind.'

Rourke shook his head, took the hand offered him and shook it. Wyndham removed his hat and sat down after he had ordered two whisky's from the bartender.

'I hope the locals are treating you well?' asked Wyndham with what seemed a genuine interest. 'Have you been down to the sale yards today? I'm told it's quite interesting for visitors to New Zealand. The Feilding stock sale is reputedly the largest in the southern hemisphere. Not bad for such a small town.'

'No I haven't been down there. I don't farm livestock but I have gathered the town is much busier than usual today but no one told me why.'

'Ah well it's not everybody's cup of tea. Bit smelly and noisy. When I first came here to work, my wife, who was at that time my employer, insisted I bid for some rams and I soon found out these local farmers are a canny lot. Paid a bit too much for them in the end. Now I leave it to Jane to do the bidding and the auctioneers are all very wary of her! One of the reasons I married her!'

'There do seem to be some formidable women around here,' commented Rourke. 'I actually came to meet Lord Sinclair but found he died a year ago so I have to deal with his daughter.'

'Yes I know what you mean. She and my wife

have become very close friends. They have a lot in common but they're both extremely good farmers. If it's agricultural advice you're looking for then you should talk to them both.'

'I farm tobacco not animals so this is new to me. Miss Sinclair was kind enough to give me a tour of the property yesterday. It was quite different to what I'd imagined.' He paused and then added, 'In several ways.'

'Did she show you her gun?' laughed Wyndham.

'Indeed she did,' muttered Keston. 'Indeed she did!'

'Well it looks as if you survived anyway. Over the years Merry has had to accomplish some very tough things and she is what she is because of that. Very brave and admirable in my opinion. Now...tell me what have you been doing with yourself? I ask because we're having a bit of a party on Saturday so why don't you come along? There'll be plenty of other farmers you can talk to. Come for dinner at seven and then more guests will arrive later and there'll be cards and dancing if that's your fancy.'

'Why thank you. That's very generous of you to invite a stranger to your home.'

Rourke meant it. The politician was friendly and at ease as he talked and gave the impression it would quite genuinely give him great pleasure to enjoy the American's company.

'All part of the job old chap,' said Wyndham. 'Between you and me it will be good to have a new face around. Do you play poker? Perhaps we can have a game?'

'Only for low stakes. I play socially that's all. My father cautioned me continually about gambling because he learned the hard way from his own mistakes. That's how he ended up in America. His father sent him there as a punishment. It's not a game I would ever pursue seriously!'

'Quite right too. We only ever bet up to £50. House rule!'

Wyndham stood and shook hands with Rourke and left him wondering if Miss Sinclair would attend this party. It was highly likely if she was such good friends with Mrs Wyndham. He looked forward to meeting her in a social situation with other guests and suddenly felt a lot happier. There might even be an opportunity to dance with her and his hands almost itched at the idea of holding her close in a waltz. It would put him in a position of control over her, perhaps the only time this would ever happen.

Later that afternoon he received another invitation in the form of a letter delivered by Merry's stable lad, asking him to come out to the farm in the morning as she had information that might interest him. He told the young man he would arrive at ten and sent him back. Perhaps the mystery of the IOU was about to be revealed because he was sure she knew far more about it than she had told him. He also had to admit to a feeling of excitement at the thought of being in her company once again and however much he told himself to stifle this emotion, he allowed himself a small grin of pleasure and hoped she would be friendlier to him than at their last parting.

So it was with high hopes that their business

could be concluded allowing him to leave Feilding that Keston presented himself at Greenleigh the next day. This time he was admitted by an elderly maid who ushered him into the drawing room and went to find Miss Sinclair. Left on his own Rourke looked around the room again. The furniture was still shabby but the room was clean and tidy and a bowl of potpourri now sat on a side table giving out a pleasant scent of rose petals and lavender as he idly sifted his fingers through it. The perfume served to make him nostalgic for his mother's house. When Merry arrived she asked him to sit down and waited in silence as the maid bought the tea things in.

'Thank you for coming out here,' she said as she poured him a cup of tea. 'I spent some time with my bank manager yesterday going back through my father's financial records. I did discover that he made a payment of £10,000 about a year and a half ago…'

'Not to my father he didn't,' interrupted Rourke knowing he sounded rude but desperate to find out what she had to tell him.

'No you're right about that but the money has gone. It was made by bank draft through an English law firm to a Mrs Findlay in Brighton. Do you know who she is because I certainly have never heard of her?'

Rourke felt a chill come over him. The name was unfamiliar but his first thoughts were that this woman must have been his father's mistress. He cleared his throat and searched desperately for the right words to explain to Lady Sinclair. It appeared he'd been made a fool of and didn't like it one little bit. But she sat there opposite him with an expression of expectancy, her lips pinched together waiting for him to say something so he swallowed hard and chose his words carefully.

'I don't recognise the name either but having said that, after he died my mother told me he had a mistress before he went to America. I can only think this must be her but he'd sworn to my mother the affair was over. For some odd reason he must have asked your father to pay her the money owing. Perhaps there was a child involved and she'd kept it secret from him for a long time.'

'The strange thing is,' said Merry. 'I never saw Papa receive any letters from your father so he must have hidden them from me somehow. I must ask my lawyer if he took delivery of letters for my father. It could be that he picked them up from there. Do you think you could be right and there was a child and that's why your father wanted to support her?'

'I have no idea. Do you have her address? Perhaps I should write to her?'

'I have the lawyer's address who dealt with the payment. But somehow I doubt if they would reveal anything to you. Perhaps if you asked them to forward a letter to her?'

Her suggestion made sense to him and he waited as she went to a desk and copied down the information from a document there.

'Here you are. No wonder my father's bank statements didn't show the payment or your father's either. The money never went into their accounts.'

Rourke rubbed his eyes and took a drink of tea trying to make sense of this. Not only was the money gone but he'd made an ass of himself in trying to claim it from an innocent woman. He searched for the right words to express this as she sat there so demurely but all his treacherous body could think of was a desire to bury his face between her beautiful breasts and beg forgiveness. He took a deep breath and banished that dream.

'Surely Lord Sinclair must have told my father the debt had been paid off. He should have torn up the IOU and then I wouldn't have embarked on this wild goose chase. I'm embarrassed beyond belief to have put you through this Miss Sinclair.'

'Well he may well have sent a letter. How are we to know after all this time?' offered Merry in a kind voice. 'My father was a heavy drinker and not at all attentive to the normal civilities. After my mother died when I was fifteen, he gradually went downhill I'm afraid and it was left to me to cope with everything as best I could. He did things that are still impacting on my life and the farm which seem totally unreasonable to me in hindsight but he thought they were for the best. I've come to reason that we cannot be responsible for our parent's shortcomings.'

Placing his tea cup back on the saucer, Rourke nodded. The mystery had been solved and he took out his wallet, removed the IOU and the deeds and handed them to his host.

'Thank you for being so understanding,' he said quietly.

'Should we have a ceremonial burning do you think?' she said with a hint of mischief in her eyes. 'Or perhaps a toast to our father's who were a couple of old reprobates by the sounds of things. God love 'em because I certainly don't!'

'I don't care what you do with them,' responded Rourke, his voice harsh. 'I feel a damn fool.'

Merry regarded him coolly, all her humour gone.

'You know if this is the worst thing to have happened to you then count yourself lucky Mr Keston. You can return home with a clear conscience knowing the debt was repaid and you've carried out your father's wishes like a good son.'

'Why don't I feel like a good son then?' he grimaced as he looked down at his hands. 'Coming here has changed everything for me.'

He gave no further explanation but Merry made a guess about his dilemma.

'Will this mean you are unable to buy land in Nelson now?'

Her question focused his mind and he shook his head.

'I didn't need the money. I was just trying to carry out my father's last wishes. I had intended to give it to my sister. She runs a school for the children on the farm and the money would have helped her to hire another teacher. Never mind at least I can say I did my best and carry on with my plans. I've been invited to attend the Wyndham's party and then I'll leave to go down south. I hope you won't think too unkindly of me. Perhaps you might even dance with me?'

They both stood and Merry took the hand he held out. He lifted it to his lips and she took a step closer and gazed up at him. He had been honest with her but she still doubted his integrity. She wanted more from him, more regret at the worry he had put her through. She did not intend to let him off quite so easily. She widened her eyes as she spoke. There would be no better chance than today offered to entice him to reveal more about himself. After the party he would be gone and she would return to reality and minding her flock.

'Storm? I shall remember you by that name and no I will never think ill of you. I understand how parents can inflict unintentional pain but I don't think you really understood what might result from your father's wishes.'

Crashing in on him came the knowledge that it would be the hardest thing to leave this woman and yet he must travel on. Her lavender scent, her soft skin and her sensuality filled him with longing. He wished he had met her under happier circumstances and not so far from his home. Now he knew it was too late to expect any sort of relationship with her. Vaguely he wondered what her childhood had been like. There had been more than a hint of bitterness in her voice when she talked about her father and he supposed it must've been hard for her growing up with no mother to guide her through the last years when the burden of running the farm fell upon her shoulders. As he looked down at her he forgot all his logical reasoning and listened to his heart, giving in to temptation and pulling her close against his chest.

'I shall miss you' he whispered. 'I wish I could stay longer and know you better.'

Merry lifted her head and gave him a knowing look with those beautiful grey eyes of hers. She ran a finger down his cheek and across his lower lip as if committing it to memory then placed her hands on his chest and bowed her head. Longing for her threaded through him and he clenched his fists to stop himself from crushing her against his body.

'I must be honest with you,' she said. 'You're the first man I've allowed to touch me since I was sixteen. I grew up with a young boy called Jack. We had a large stable of horses then because my father used to race them at the Feilding racecourse. He was mad for anything he could gamble on. Jack was the stable manager's son and I suppose we were like two puppies playing together from the moment we were toddlers.'

'Jack was two years older than me, like an older brother until I was fifteen and he was seventeen. I suppose you could say we explored each other with a natural curiosity. But of course we were sure we loved each other and Jack asked my father if we could get married. Of course he said no and sent Jack away. A few months later my father told me Jack had gone down to the goldfields in Otago and been killed in a mining accident. He said a sluice collapsed and several miners drowned as they were swept down the hillside. Life was never the same after that. It was only the fact that I was forced to start running the farm and taking charge when my father relapsed into his drinking affliction that kept me going. Somehow I've managed to stay single but that hasn't meant that I didn't want a husband. But somehow no-one ever saw me like that. I was always good old Merry striding around in the mud as if I were a man instead of meekly sitting and doing embroidery. Not wife material apparently although plenty have wanted to sleep with me!'

Rourke held her close and considered what she said. He found it hard to believe she hadn't been courted. He ran his hands down her back wanting the gesture to be comforting but instead it had the opposite effect on him. The warmth of her body as she leaned into him was the catalyst for his arousal and an overwhelming sense of lust seized him.

Merry could feel the effect she was having on Rourke and alarm bells went off in her head. Bloody hell, it was the same every time a man had tried to flirt with her over the years since Jack had possessed her. It had not happened at the picnic but then she reasoned she had been in control and Keston had been restrained. Why couldn't she just give into her desires and take pleasure from this man? Would she always be afraid of the consequences? Now, however, she knew he was very close to overcoming her best intentions and whilst she found him almost irresistible, it was only almost...Self preservation had become ingrained in her mind over the years.

'Mr Keston, please let me go?' she demanded, trying to make her voice strong and formal, as she attempted to push him away with all her strength. 'This won't do sir.'

He stood back from her but held on to her hands as if they were a lifeline to her, his thumbs smoothing and soothing her skin.

'Why? You want me as much as I want you. Don't deny it. At the picnic I practically had to fight you off!'

Merry gasped at this point of view.

'I believe it was you who tried to get inside my shirt by pointing out my loose button. You could have simply told me but no you had to touch me.'

'And very touchable you are my Merry. I wanted to touch you all over but even I knew that was never going to happen. But now we know each other a little better I think?'

'Well you think wrong sir!'

Ignoring her protest, he pulled her hard against him and kissed her. Merry stiffened at first until his tongue teased her lips and demanded they open. He tasted so sweet she succumbed to his entry and allowed him to stir her senses in a way that had never happened to her before. She wound her arms round his back as his mouth moved down to her neck and his hands caressed her backside. Before she could stop him he pushed her down on to the settee and kneeling he lifted her skirts and ran his hands over her thighs before gently pushing them apart to reach the softness between her legs.

'You're so beautiful, so tempting, ' he whispered and bent his head to kiss her most sensitive and intimate place with such skill she jerked upwards as the fire created by his touch ran through her body. She clung on to his shoulders as his fingers explored her folds and she felt them slide into her body and plunge deep, prolonging the ecstasy of her passionate response to his tongue. This was far from the juvenile probing and fumbling she had thought so wonderful from Jack. This was a man skilled with the art of bringing a woman immense pleasure and she moaned as he slid his fingers out of her. Lifting her head she watched as he started to unfasten his trousers and suddenly she came back to reality.

'No! No!' she shouted at him. 'Enough. No further please.'

Rourke looked at her, his face suddenly hard as she pulled her skirts down and tried to move away from him. He put his hands on her hips and held her down and she saw his eyes narrow.

'I didn't take you for a cockteaser Merry Sinclair.'

His crude and cruel remark hit hard like a blow to her stomach and she wrenched his hands off her, shoved him backwards so he fell on the floor. As she stood, he crouched on the carpet fixing her with an expression of disbelief and she moved to leave the room. But she only got as far as the door before she was grabbed, swung round and slammed back against it. Rourke held her there, shaking with fury.

'I think I deserve an explanation,' he ground out. 'I'm not leaving until you tell me why you stopped me.'

It was no use trying to appeal to his gentlemanly instincts because it was obvious he did not possess any if she judged correctly. This was a man who had no qualms about taking her money or her farm from her, a man who thought she was fair game, his for his own pleasure no doubt. Honesty had to be her best policy here.

'Before you lost your head,' she said with great bitterness. 'You might recall I said I have no objections to finding a husband but I have no intention of taking a lover. That way is full of danger. If I had let you have your way I could have ended up pregnant and you would have left me to continue your travels.  Understand that under those circumstances I would never carry a child for you. I would get rid of it as soon as I knew it existed. I couldn't go through...' she stopped as he released her and stood back. Then she continued, 'You would never have gained my farm because my father mortgaged it up to the maximum the bank would lend him, nearly the full value. Even if you sold it, all the money would have to be paid to the bank. I've been trying to pay it back little by little but even so it will be many years before I'm debt free. You were so lucky that my father repaid that loan because it would have been sweet revenge to hand the farm to you knowing it really belongs to the bank.'

'There's no trust between us then? Were you ever intending to tell me?' he almost hissed at her and Merry shook her head. 'Very well then, I'd better leave. I can only say I had no intention of raping or ruining you. I've never got any woman with child and would have taken every care with you. But I have a feeling you won't believe me somehow.' He bit his lips together and surveyed her sadly. 'I hoped...' he paused then gently put her aside and left the room.

Still breathing hard Merry smoothed down her skirt and then went to the window and watched as he mounted his horse and trotted away down the drive. He never looked back and she put her hand on her heart as she fought down tears. There must be no regret on her part for the way she had treated him. She had taken a huge risk once in her life with disastrous consequences and it would never happen again she vowed. There would be no man in her life unless marriage was promised and delivered.

## CHAPTER 12

Rourke pushed his mount hard on the return to Feilding. Part of him knew he had approached Merry in entirely the wrong way. Who could blame her for wishing to see him get his come-uppance? He had barged into her home thinking she was a servant and issued his ultimatum with no regard for her circumstances. Admittedly he was an exceptionally hard man in business dealings but never with women. What was it about this particular one that brought out the pompous ass in him? His conscience told him it was because she stood up to him, spoke to him as an equal and was not one bit fooled by him. His mother was a sweet Southern lady who had been raised to please her husband and provide children and while she could be defiant it had never caused his father any trouble as far as he knew. Merry Sinclair was built of much sterner stuff and while he found this admirable he also found it baffled him. On the one hand she had seemed open to dalliance and on the other she had all the characteristics of a prudish spinster.

He sighed as he reached the livery stable and gave his horse to the stable lad. There was no point in becoming attached to a woman who did not reciprocate his feelings and the sooner he resumed his plans the better. But all the same after he entered his hotel room and pulled off his riding boots, he threw himself on the bed and indulged in a fit of pique that soon turned to anger at his own lack of self control. If only he had wooed her slowly...But the very thought of this began to conjure up visions of weddings and children and he quickly shunted those thoughts away. It was only lust he felt for Merry he told himself firmly, just a physical need that he could deal with if necessary. He would forgo the party at the Wyndham's, send them a note of apology and make his way down to the South Island. Yes that was the best idea and nothing would change his mind. It would be unbearable to be in the same house as Merry let alone the same room and as for having to stand by and watch her dance with other men, he simply did not have to place himself in that position. He had to stop thinking about holding her close as they waltzed, inhaling her wonderful scent and gazing down only to find all his senses drowning in her beautiful expressive eyes. Looking up at the ceiling he could almost hear the music and laughter and with a groan he sat up and hauled himself upright before reaching for the whisky on his nightstand and taking a long swig straight from the bottle. But in his head there was only one recurrent thought about the lady. Mine. Mine. Mine.

## CHAPTER 13

Merry seriously considered not attending the Wyndham party but she had no wish to upset Jane after all her kindness. The original idea of holding the event had been to encourage Rourke Keston to soften his attitude to her but that opportunity was long over now the mystery of the IOU had been solved and especially after their argument yesterday. Perhaps she could have been a little less unpleasant to him but then again, she had a great deal more to lose from a brief affair than he did. No it was best she called a halt when she did and surely she would soon recover from the passionate emotions he evoked in her. It was unlikely he would attend the party now she told herself as she packed a few overnight things and set off in the dogcart for Totara Hills.

At her destination she was welcomed by Jane who appeared to be in command of dozens of servants rushing hither and thither. Large flower arrangements decorated the rooms and last minute details were being addressed. Throughout the house preparations were at full swing.

'It's grown from just a few chums to rather a large do,' explained Jane quite apologetically as she wove her way purposefully through waiters and maids. 'I never realised we knew so many people who had to be invited according to Gareth but I daresay it will all work well in the end. Thank goodness I managed to limit the dinner guests to twenty. As it is we'll be rubbing elbows with each other even with the extension in the dining table.'

Merry thought of Bessy, labouring hard in the kitchen and wondered how she was coping but on the other hand knew this was a woman who could spit roast a whole cattle beast and have it perfectly cooked without a qualm. Jane led the way upstairs and down a long passage way finally opening a door into a pleasant bedroom.

'There you are Merry. We've just installed a boiler downstairs so there's a bathroom right next door with nice hot running water. Please help yourself when you are ready. Emma has hung your dress in the wardrobe and will come and help you dress. Come down at six o'clock and we'll have drinks before dinner. I expect you'll know everyone so no need to feel shy!'

With a wave she disappeared back into the corridor and Merry was left on her own.  She had rather hoped to tell Jane about her encounter with Rourke but her hostess was too involved with the party preparations. It was hardly fair to expect Jane to drop everything to listen to her pathetic tale. She unpacked her overnight things and went to the window. The room overlooked a beautiful garden and to her right she could see the roof of the new house extensions Gareth had built. There was a ballroom, a billiard room and a new office for him matching the white painted boards of the rest of the house and a massive glass conservatory crammed with tropical plants from orchids to palm trees. How she wished she had this sort of money to spend on her own home. It was not that she begrudged the Wyndham's their wealth. They had both worked extremely hard for it but it was becoming increasingly difficult to maintain her own homestead with the small income she had to live on.

One could only hope that the wool prices would lift in the future and then she would rejoice in giving her home a fresh coat of paint and fixing some of the leaks in the roof. As she stood here it occurred to her how hard her life was compared to Jane's but then her friend had arrived here wealthy and already owning her land which made all the difference.

It was no use standing here dreaming of what might be or what might have been, she had a ball to prepare herself for and suddenly she started to feel quite excited at the prospect of wearing a beautiful dress. Perhaps there might be someone here tonight who thought she was interesting and worthwhile. It was no use wishing that Rourke was coming when she was quite certain he was already on his way to Wellington. It seemed a good time to go and explore this beautiful new bathroom Jane had told her about. Perhaps if she could lie in hot scented water it would sooth the ache she felt every time she thought about him.

## CHAPTER 14

Later, when Merry left her room, she had to pluck up the courage to descend the staircase as she heard laughter and talking coming from the drawing room. Emma had come to help her dress and her hair was swept up on top of her head with a few curls falling around her shoulders. She resisted the urge to sweep them back as they tended to tickle her skin but she held her head high and entered the room as if she was used to such occasions. Luckily Jane spotted her and came across the room and took her arm.

'Let me introduce you to Sir William and Lady Fox. They've come up from Wellington to spend the weekend at their house Westoe just over the river from Halcombe. They're spending the night here too.'

Merry was presented to the couple who she recalled because Sir William had been the first Premier in the New Zealand government. Now retired, he still played an active part in politics. They chatted about the weather and the gardens at their home which were full of beautiful specimen trees and plants that Sir William had gathered from all over the world. Once again Merry marvelled at what one could do if one had money but she was too polite to mention this. Catching sight of another farmer she knew she made her excuses to the Foxes and moved further into the room.

All went well as she became more at ease and she found that sipping her sherry helped a great deal too. She was just convincing herself that this would be a most enjoyable evening when she sensed someone behind her and the warmth of a large hand on her waist made her spin round. Rourke Keston smiled down at her and her confidence shattered into tiny pieces.

'Miss Sinclair, a pleasure to meet you again,' he said politely even as his hand pressed harder against the bodice of her gown with a possessiveness she felt must be obvious to everyone who watched. 'May I compliment you on how beautiful you look tonight.'

He was drunk, she was quite sure of it, yet his gaze was steady as he looked down at her and she found it hard to avoid the hungry look in his eyes. Mustering all her strength she backed away from him to place a more acceptable distance between them.

'Mr Keston, I'm very surprised to see you. I was quite sure you would be well on your way to the capital by now?'

She congratulated herself on how cool she sounded in case anyone was listening but she knew he would not be deceived. What on earth was he doing here and how had he gathered the nerve to come and talk to her? Now she would have to spend the rest of the night trying to avoid him. It seemed so unfair but then she was resigned to nothing in her life being fair so far. This was quite normal for her but she was still very surprised and discomfited by his presence. He was dressed all in black, even his shirt and some part of her wanted to ask him irreverently if he was going to a funeral because it certainly felt as if she was now he had arrived. She lowered her eyes and focused on his hands, noticing the cufflinks shining against his dark shirt. They looked like tiny gold nuggets.

'Changed my mind Miss Sinclair,' he drawled. 'Fancied myself a bit of a hoedown, as we call it back home. It's been a long time since I kicked up my heels!'

Luckily the gong for dinner went and Merry sought escape but Rourke offered her his arm and propriety made her accept. He tucked her hand close against his body and for a few brief seconds she enjoyed this shared intimate moment. It was with relief that she found her place at the long dining table and saw that Rourke would be sitting on the other side, considerably further down where he would not be able to enter into any conversation with her. She was so glad she had asked Jane to rearrange the seating in case he turned up. Even so she found herself perversely longing to talk to him but instead carried on an earnest conversation with a farmer on her left about wool prices. To her right sat a young man who had recently started an accountancy business in town and gradually she managed to draw him out about his ambitions.

She learned his name was Thomas Wheeler and after he had taken two glasses of wine he became a great deal more vivacious and less serious. He put his arm along the back of her chair in a very intimate fashion while they were waiting for dessert to be served and Merry gave him a smile before she looked down the table and found Rourke Keston frowning at her. This only made her double her efforts to have a thoroughly stimulating discussion with Thomas about double entry book keeping a subject she found extremely boring but still managed to look as if it was the most exciting thing she'd heard about for years.

'Many of my clients find this too difficult to

understand,' commented Mr Wheeler. 'It's very gratifying to find someone who can grasp the concept.'

He raised his glass to her and leaned a little closer. It seemed worthwhile to Merry to keep the conversation going and she laughed girlishly at the young accountant hoping it would upset Rourke. At the same time she admitted to herself it was childish of her to try and provoke jealousy in a man she had no interest in. Definitely no interest at all! She must remember to keep telling herself that.

'I've had to keep my farm ledgers for years now so I have a good knowledge of figures, not that mine are very exciting. But it is a very important part of farming these days. One must know where the pennies are being spent at all times,' she offered to keep his interest going fully aware of the even stormier looks that were coming her way from the American.

'Perhaps you would consider allowing me to do your bookkeeping,' suggested the young accountant. 'That would give you more time to work on your farm. If I may so bold as to say I think I would find the thought of your figures most exciting!'

'Yes indeed it would allow me more time,' agreed Merry with another slightly foolish giggle that sounded flirtatious and false to her ears. 'But unfortunately as I said my income is quite meagre and I'm afraid I couldn't afford to pay anyone to do my books.'

Thomas Wheeler flushed and said hastily,' I don't think there's anything wrong with your figure Miss Sinclair.' Then he coughed loudly.' I do apologise, I shouldn't have said that. Of course I meant to say your *figures*.'

Merry laughed genuinely as she watched his embarrassment and she patted him on the hand just to add fuel to the fire for both the men who seemed so interested in her tonight.

'Of course you did and I'm not at all offended. That's a very nice compliment,' she said. 'And I get so few these days.'

'Perhaps we could have a dance later on,' Thomas asked.' I promise to try very hard not to tread on your toes.'

'That would be lovely,' responded Merry and then she turned to the farmer on the left so that she could lift her eyes and watch Keston watching her.

Once dinner was finished Gareth announced there would be card games for those who were interested or dancing to a small musical ensemble of strings and a piano. Thomas offered his arm to Merry and led her into the new ballroom where he steered her carefully around the floor, so much so that she could almost hear him counting under his breath. When the music finished she thanked him and he led her back to a group of chairs set against the wall but she didn't have a chance to sit down before she noticed Keston arrive at her side.

'Miss Sinclair may I have the honour ma'am?' There was no way she could deny him as people all around her were watching the tall American with his unusual manners and dress. He took her hand as she nodded her agreement and drew her into his arms as the music started again and Merry experienced a strange sensation of being exactly where she should be.

And being with the one person who made her happy. To the strains of violins, he led her across the floor with impeccable timing and an elegant grace that she would never have guessed at. She hardly dared to look up at his face because she knew instinctively he had hardly taken his eyes off her once they started dancing. As they progressed she felt him pulling her closer until there was barely a space between their bodies and she was almost overwhelmed by the subtle scent of the citrus shaving cream that lingered on his skin as he bent his head to speak to her.

'Don't look so frightened,' he whispered in her ear. 'I'm not going to eat you much as I love the taste of you!'

A burst of heat exploded through her body at his comment. She looked around as if hoping for rescue but no-one appeared to notice her scarlet cheeks. There was nothing she could do short of resorting to begging him. She would not cause a scene at her friend's party however much she wished to slap Keston's lecherous smile from his face. Or did she? Her body yearned for any contact with him, violent or passionate even while her mind tried to remain cool and distant. So begging it would have to be.

'Please behave yourself Rourke,' she pleaded. 'Remember these are my neighbours and I meet with them regularly. I don't need any scandalous behavior. There was enough of that when my father was alive. You can walk away tomorrow and not worry about any gossip but I don't have that perogative.'

'No,' he whispered in her ear, his breath teasing her neck. 'I have absolutely no intention of conforming.

Good behaviour is the last thing on my mind tonight. Can I see you home later?

"No I'm staying here overnight,' said Merry, relieved that she could offer a genuine excuse to keep him away from her.

'Which room is yours?'

The sheer audacity of his question forced her to look at him and she almost stopped breathing as she endured the wickedness of his smile. Lust for this tall strong man flooded through her. She couldn't deny it and she was immensely glad the music suddenly ended and she could step back from him and be spared this impossible conversation. However before she could leave him he once again possessively tucked her hand into his arm and drew her out of the ballroom back into the drawing room where the card tables had been set up.

'I feel lucky tonight,' he said, smiling down at her. 'Come and watch me play.'

Gareth Wyndham waved out to them and beckoned them over to a round table set in the bay window and Merry was forced towards it with her dancing partner as he would not release her arm.

'Keston do you fancy a round of poker? I've heard all you Americans are very expert at it. It's a game Jane and I love to play but we don't often get the chance. Shall we make up a foursome? Will you play Merry?'

'Of course she will,' said Jane appearing at his side. Another embarrassing moment passed for Merry and she looked to her friends for support. They knew full well she had no money to gamble with but Jane gave her a huge wink, walked close to her and pressed a roll of notes into her friend's hand while Gareth deliberately distracted Keston. Merry nodded her thanks, put the money discreetly into her reticule and sat down at the table. She understood perfectly what Jane was up to.

'I'll be bank,' offered Jane. 'The stakes are a pound a chip up to £50.'

The three players put their money on the table and Jane counted out the chips to each of them. She shuffled the cards expertly and started to deal. A waiter came over and poured whisky for the two men but Mary declined a sherry and carefully lifted her cards before dropping them back on the table. Keston looked at his cards too, his face remaining impassive and Jane smiled. Merry and Gareth looked worried. More bets were placed and cards dealt and then Gareth folded. Keston watched Merry closely but she gave nothing away and he doubled his bet and she followed his action.

'I'll see you,' he said but regretted this as she laid the winning hand down and pulled all the chips towards her. Jane clapped, Gareth smiled while Keston looked disgruntled.

'Just beginners  luck,' said Merry with a grin. 'Deal them again Jane. I'm certain Mr Keston will win his money back this time. It's been such a long time since I played this game I'm sorely out of practice.'

Four games later Keston was nearly out of chips and nearly tearing his hair out. Despite good hands he hadn't won a single game and it was obvious that Merryweather Sinclair was a dab hand at poker and somehow the Wyndham's had set him up. He watched as Merry put £75 in her reticule and then passed the remaining £75 over to Jane.

'She wins for me every time Mr Keston. We split the difference. Never play her at whist. Merry can count the cards every time,' Jane chuckled and he was forced to concede they had fooled him very neatly.

'My father taught me,' Merry told him almost sounding apologetic. 'And when he started drinking so heavily I played endless games with him hoping it would distract him.'

The lack of bitterness in her voice spoke of endless patience with Lord Sinclair and Rourke doubted if he would have been able to muster the same apparent indifference if he had been in a similar position. Here was a young woman who had been left almost destitute but survived by her own sheer hard work. But this was not the occasion to question her and he had to remind himself the chance might never arise between them and he strove to keep their conversation light hearted and sociable.

'Well I suppose practice makes perfect,' said Rourke. 'But next time I'd prefer you were my partner in a game rather than the opposition. I sense you've had your revenge once again on me tonight.'

'We might play very well together... but unfortunately, as you're most likely leaving tomorrow it won't be possible.'

Her flat statement brought it home to him again that after tonight it was very likely he would never see her or the Wyndham's again and suddenly he felt bereft. There was something about these people and this place that felt like home. How easy it would be to stay, but then there was no guarantee he could establish himself around here. Pushing his chair back Rourke gazed around the room and decided to ask Merry for one more dance, something to create a memory that he could hold close to him on all the lonely nights he knew now would fill the rest of his life without this woman.

'May I have another dance?' he asked her as she stood and smoothed down her skirts. She nodded and without another word took his arm and let him lead her back into the ballroom. Even though the floor was crowded they managed to dance more formally than before with Rourke holding her lightly around the waist as her gloved hand rested in his. Merry was certain he must be able to feel to feel the trembling that beset her whole body even though she attempted to hold herself quite stiffly. Just the warmth of his breath on her cheek as he bent his head to look at her, was enough to set her senses reeling. When the music ended he kept hold of her for a few seconds then reluctantly released her and stood back.

'I'd better leave soon before the moon disappears. I don't enjoy riding in the dark on a strange road.'

Merry nodded and fought back tears. How foolish to find how much he meant to her when it was too late. Her mind searched for an opportunity to keep a link with him.

'I'd appreciate it if you would write and let me know who the mysterious Mrs Finlay is? '

'Yes of course I will,' he responded and she was

certain she detected a slight hint of eagerness in his voice as if he was glad to do this. 'I would like to correspond with you anyway. Would that be acceptable?'

Her lips trembled and he clenched his fists at his side in an effort not to reach out to her in this crowded room. How was he going to tear himself away in a few moments?

'Please write. Please,' was all she said before spinning away and walking out of his sight leaving him keenly aware of the tremor in her voice.

Two days later Keston stood on the waterfront in Wellington looking out over the harbor, trying to rally his enthusiasm for the voyage down to Nelson. It was the last place on earth he wished to visit at this precise moment. Would his life tumble into chaos if he did not carry out his plans? It was already fundamentally altered by the emotions he now endured after parting with Merry. Looking around at the busy wharf he wondered what would happen if he abandoned his plans? There was still time to change his mind he decided and taking a deep breath, he made his way to the shipping office, his priorities altered.

## CHAPTER 15

The shearers had nearly finished clipping all the sheep and Merry stretched her back as she leaned her broom against the wool press. They had worked hard for nearly a week now with the early December weather fine and warm. A satisfying number of heavy bales bulging with clean wool had been stacked ready for sale and she relished the thought of rising commodity prices bringing her some extra income to help pay a bit more off the mortgage.

As the last animal was shorn and pushed down the chute to escape into the yards outside, the shearers started to pack their gear ready to move on to the next job. The head man gave her the tallies and she was pleased to see not too many sheep had been lost since the last count six months before. The region had suffered a wet and bitterly cold winter and the lambing season had been poor with exposure to the elements just too much for many of the young animals.

Her hands were blistered from seven days sweeping all the fleeces clear of the shearing board and not for the first time, she regretted not wearing gloves for the job. Never mind it was finished now and all she had to do was tidy the shed and then she could go back to the house for a bath. Her hair and skin were impregnated with the smell of lanolin from the raw wool she had been handling. Even with the help of her two shepherds it had been physically hard mustering the sheep into the wool shed pens as the shearers methodically worked their way through the mob of well over a thousand animals.

Merry welcomed the hard physical work which dulled her senses and exhausted her. She welcomed the deep dreamless sleep that overtook her every night during shearing before rising at dawn to face another day without Rourke. For the first few weeks after he left she replayed their last evening together constantly as soon as she tried to sleep. Could she have persuaded him to stay longer? Had she missed any clues in their conversation that might have given her a deeper insight into his character? Why was she wasting so much time in speculating on something that was clearly not meant to be? Her nights were grim, she tossed and turned and burned for him with no glimmer of hope.

Later that night, after she ate her evening meal in the kitchen, she was almost asleep but determined to write up her farm records while the week's progress was fresh in her mind. Tomorrow she would go into Feilding and arrange for the wool merchant to come out to Greenleigh and load the bales for transporting for sale at the auction in Wellington. Fingers crossed the payment would be in her bank account in a few weeks. Perhaps even in time to give her loyal staff a small Christmas bonus?

Her desk was not as cluttered as it had been a few months ago. Due to her financial situation she had cancelled subscriptions to her farming journals and the newspaper. A weekly visit to the library helped her keep up to date with any information she required but she had to admit it wasn't the same as sitting with her own personal copies. Idly she looked through the post but there was nothing of interest. Rourke Keston had never written as he promised and by now the ache in her heart had been subdued a little even if she did think of him a great deal too much when she wasn't busy. It was over a year since his departure before last Christmas and she imagined he was well settled back in West Virgina and probably married as well although why she tortured herself with that concept was a mystery to her.

The Wyndham's had ceased asking her if she had heard from him and it was generally accepted he had forgotten all about them once returned to America. With a sigh Merry found her paper knife and slit open the envelope containing her latest bank statement. Quickly looking at the balance she gasped and checked that she had received the correct account. The statement showed her mortgage figure had been paid off and she was in the black. There was no explanation as to where the money had come from but it was obvious to her someone in the bank had made a huge error in typing out the sheet. That was the only explanation. She was certain she had not come into some secret inheritance and there was no rich relative to come to her rescue. Ah well she would have to visit the bank manager tomorrow and point out the mistake although she did briefly wonder if she could ignore it for a while just to enjoy the pleasure of reading this statement. Perhaps she would frame it, mistake or not and she giggled out loud at this idea. It was, she thought, the first time she had laughed out loud for a very long time.

The winter had taken a terrible toll on her farm. Constant rain had brought down landslides on many of the back hills revealing escarpments of raw clay disfiguring the landscape. The ewes dragged themselves over the paddocks searching for grass that refused to grow in the cold weather and Merry had lost count of the number of dead lambs she and her shepherds had picked up. Her wool shed had been full of ewes tied up with orphan lambs mothered on to them if they had lost their own. One wet day after another took its toll on Merry too and she had actually sunk to her knees in a pen one day and resting her head against the damp softness of a ewe, fallen asleep for a few blissful minutes until the animal had moved. It seemed she was constantly muddy and dragging herself around in heavy oilskins.

Now she was grateful to be facing summer and to forget for a while the whole cycle which would start again in six months time. She looked forward to improved weather and the chance to spend time in the garden.

## CHAPTER 16

It was with a profound feeling of relief that Merry arrived home the next day from Feilding after arranging the sale of her wool. However her trip to the bank had provided no conclusion about the mystery deposit in her account. Mr Brownlee the manager was not available and the clerk was less than helpful.

'I'm sorry Miss Sinclair,' he said. 'It was a private transaction and I'm not allowed to look at those ledgers without Mr Brownlee's permission. I'm afraid you'll have to wait till he comes back but I have to speculate that it's not a mistake. Mr Brownlee checks all the statements before they're sent out and he would never have missed something like that if it was incorrect. It's so obvious, a significant sum.'

Merry was forced to accept she would have to wait a few more days to find out the truth of the matter and she went home feeling frustrated that she had been unable to discover where this mystery payment came from. She guided the dog cart up the driveway and round the back to the stables and went inside through the kitchen. In the hallway she unpinned her hat and took off her gloves before she hung her coat on the hall stand.

Just about to go into the drawing room for a cup of tea she heard a knock on the front door and opened it to find a ghost facing her. A tall, lean, dark blond headed man, who smiled and said,' Good day Merry.'

She clutched her mouth to stop herself crying out and then gasped in astonishment.

'Jack is that you? I thought you were dead!'

The man laughed and Merry was left in no doubt that Jack Fisher had returned to her alive and well. Without thinking she reached out and touched his arm to reassure herself he was real and then reached out to him in an embrace that expressed all her joy and amazement at his appearance. She laughed and she cried and suddenly her life did not seem so bad after all.

'I'm sorry to give you such a shock then,' he said when they had finally managed to draw apart. 'I know it's been a long, long time but I came to Palmerston North to visit my father and I felt I owed it to you to come and see how you were.'

'I'm so glad you did. Please come in Jack. I'll get over my surprise in a minute.'

She led him into the drawing room and rang the bell to ask the maid to put an extra cup and saucer with the tea things. Jack Fisher had aged well and had grown from a skinny seventeen year-old to a mature man, broad in the shoulders and well-dressed. He sat down opposite her as she poured the tea and she still couldn't stop looking at him. There were just so many questions flying around her head she didn't know where to start.

'Why did you think I was dead?'

'Because that's what my father told me. After you'd been gone a few months he said he'd heard it in the pub. He said a sluice at the goldmine had collapsed and several miners had been drowned including you. Later I saw a newspaper report about the accident but it didn't give any names and I had no reason to disbelieve him. So what did happen to you the last ten years? I can't wait to hear.'

Jack took the cup and saucer and collected his thoughts. Hearing that Lord Sinclair was dead, this news had convinced him to visit Greenleigh and see whether Merry was still living here. He had been almost certain she would have been married by now but he noticed she wore no rings.

'Your father was a hard man. I'll never forget how vitriolic he was towards me when I asked to marry you. He gave me no chance to say goodbye to you. He actually stood over me with his shotgun and watched as I packed my bag and left. My father followed me two weeks later because he was so furious at my treatment. We stayed at my aunt's house over in Palmerston North. Father got a job at the racecourse as head stable manager and I decided to go down to Otago and try my hand at gold mining. But it wasn't for me. I didn't last very long, not much more than two weeks!' He gave a laugh at his own foolishness. 'I ended up in Christchurch working as a barman in a big hotel and after two years I married the owner's daughter. Then he died and left the place to my wife and I. We have two sons and we've done very well. In the meantime my father married a widow and they were very happy. Sadly she died recently and I decided to come to the funeral because it's been so many years since I've seen my father. We wrote but not frequently but now he's decided to travel back with me to Christchurch and be a grandfather which is wonderful.'

Merry listened and felt a great sense of relief to hear all had ended well for her first love. She was even glad to hear of his marriage and children even though this saddened her in many ways she would have to explain to him.

'All these years Jack and I've believed you dead and you were creating a good life for yourself. I'm so glad for you truly. In hindsight we were much too young to be married.'

'I heard your father died.'

'Yes he died over two years ago now. He was a very bitter man towards the end of his life and I must be honest and say it was a relief when he passed away. He was in a great deal of pain, he was very stubborn and refused to see a doctor and all of us here suffered because of that. He and my mother are buried together upon the back hill.'

'And you Merry? Are you married?'

Jack's face was filled with kindness which nearly brought tears to Merry's eyes. It was so long since anyone had asked about her.

'No. My father left everything in such a state I've spent all these years working to improve the farm.' Her words were carefully chosen. 'There hasn't been much time for social events or courting even if a man had come along that I liked.'

'Are you telling me that no local man has tried to woo you? You're even more beautiful now than you were at fifteen. I suppose we've both grown up a great deal.'

His words were genuine and she thought how lucky his wife was have such a fine husband but she didn't feel jealous. The time for regret was long over now and instead she felt quite sisterly towards him.

'There was one man a year ago but he was only visiting New Zealand. He lives in America and he had to return.'

'Then he must've been a bloody fool,' said Jack vehemently.

'No he wasn't foolish. I discouraged him for various reasons that I'll tell you about later. Now would you like to ride up through the farm for old time's sake? I'll show you some of the changes I've been able to put in place since you left. We had a terrible winter and there's a great deal of damage and repairs to be done now the weather has improved.'

Jack nodded and they made their way out stables and set off to revive some old memories of their childhood.

## CHAPTER 17

Had it really been a year since that first time he had passed through the gates of Greenleigh? Rourke Keston halted his horse at the bottom of the driveway and took a deep breath. Would Merry Sinclair welcome him or would she treat him with disdain? He was uncertain how to approach her but meet her he must to put right the animosity between them and endeavour to replace it with something much more worthwhile. Over the past months he had been constantly reminded of her and how his feelings had changed so rapidly in the short time he knew her. In fact he had come to appreciate how she had taken advantage of him when she knew full well her farm could never be his. Maybe he should have guessed when she took his arrival and demands so calmly that there was a secret she was withholding from him. It struck him that he had never been so naive where a woman was concerned and if she rejected him today he only had himself to blame. But he'd gone too far by now and burned his bridges so he rode forward up to the house, dismounted and hitched his horse by the front steps. His knock on the door was answered by the elderly maid who peered at him as if he was a ghost.

'Mr Keston we weren't expecting you,' she greeted him and ushered him into the hallway.

'Is Miss Sinclair at home?'

'No I believe she just went for a ride up to the back of the farm. You might like to follow her.'

There was something in the way she smiled at

him which made him feel uneasy but he nodded and went back out to mount his horse. As he rode over the farm he started to feel quite nervous about the approaching meeting with Merry and slowed his horse to a walk as they entered into a group of trees. Just as he was about to come out into the open again he looked up the hillside towards the grave yard and what he saw caused him to pull his horse to an abrupt halt.

In the distance he could see Merry and a tall well-built man standing beside each other inside the picket fence that surrounded the graves. There was something intimate in the way they appeared. As he watched they knelt and were hidden by the grave stones. After a few moments they both stood up and the man took Merry in his arms and pulled her close, her head resting on his chest. The couple stood quietly like this for a few moments then he released her and they left the graveyard, mounted their horses and came down the track towards Rourke. He hastily turned his horse and drew back amongst the tree as they rode past him. Both seemed sunk in their thoughts and never noticed him watching them.

When they were safely passed and out of sight, Rourke rode up the hill to the graveyard. His mind was spinning with questions. What had they been looking at? Who was the man so familiar with Merry that he could hold her in such a close embrace? Had she married since he left? Rourke dismounted and opened the gate into the cemetery. He looked at the headstones and then down at his feet where he judged the couple had been standing. A single red rose had been laid on a small bronze tablet set in the grass.

He bent to read the inscription. '*Alexander Sinclair Fisher, born March 5th 1886, died March 7th 1886, our beloved son an angel now in heaven.*'

Rourke read this information again and then looked the headstones where Merry's mother was buried. She had died well before this baby was born. Now he understood why Merry had such a deep attachment to this farm and why she had been so terrified of becoming pregnant again. This was her child buried here. He bowed his head, his thoughts racing and all he could think of was returning to the house and talking to her about this tragic event she had endured in her very young life. How had she survived without a mother to support her? He had a young sister of his own but she had married a good man and had family around her when their children were born. Had Lord Sinclair helped his daughter? But then he recalled Fisher had been sent away possibly before she knew she was pregnant.

Keston remembered nothing about the ride back to Greenleigh. The maid let him in again and gestured to the drawing where he could hear voices. He opened the door and found Merry and the man he had seen her with before sitting opposite each other deep in conversation. As she noticed him he experienced a gut wrenching spasm travelling through his whole body. The shock in her eyes and then the sudden realisation that the maid had not mentioned his arrival all served to ram home to him how much he loved her. He had missed her unceasingly and now he was determined no other man would take her away from him as long as he breathed. He noticed the visitor stand slowly but he ignored him and walked towards Merry who sat frozen as he approached but finally stood holding out her hands slowly. He took them in his, bent his head and pressed his mouth to her warm skin dimly aware of the man watching him keenly.

Merry could not believe that Keston had come back to her and she fought to find the right words to greet him. She started trembling as his lips traced over her hands and she breathed in the warm scent of him, leather, horses and musk. With a huge effort she pulled herself together, remembered her manners and looked between the two men.

'Rourke! This is such a surprise. May I introduce Jack Fisher? Jack this is Mr Keston.'

Jack shook Rourke's hand with a query in his eyes but the American spoke first his voice harsh and almost accusatory.

'Aren't you supposed to be dead, Fisher?'

'Apparently so,' said Jack with a grin that showed no offence at the blunt comment. 'But fortunately for me the rumours of my demise are not true.'

'You've waited a long time to come back and discount them?' stated Rourke. 'Can I take it you didn't know that Miss Sinclair had been told you were killed?'

'No, I had no idea and if I had I would have written straight away. We were both so young then. It's easy now, in hindsight to know I should have stood up for myself against her father but he threatened me and saw me off the property with his shotgun. I'd no idea what had happened to her. If I had I would never have left her.'

At this point Mary felt she had to interrupt these confessions but before she could say anything Jack came up to her and gave her a chaste kiss on the cheek.

'I must go. I have to ride back to the city and my father before it gets dark. I think from what you've told me, you and Mr Keston must have much to talk about,' and he gave her a slow wink which reminded her so much of the cheeky boy he had been all those years ago.

'Thank you for coming back Jack. It's meant a great deal to me. Perhaps if I have to visit Christchurch I'll come and stay with you.'

She took his hand and squeezed it and Rourke agonised over the affectionate way she looked at him.

'I'll see myself out the back way,' said Jack. 'I think you'd better stay with your visitor. I don't want any farewell tears Merry. Take care of yourself.'

And he was gone leaving Merry and Rourke staring at each other until she remembered her manners and gestured for him to sit down.

'So that was the famous Jack Fisher, your long lost love?'

Rourke hated the bitterness in his tone and smiled at her in an effort to soften his comment. He could sense she was near tears but her next words were almost defiant.

'Before we go any further, I should tell you that he's happily married with three children. He owns a hotel in Christchurch. He seems to have done very well for himself. I can't believe what a dreadful man my father turned out to be. I must've been so naive to believe everything he told me. It just seems to go on getting worse.'

Rourke leaned towards her, caring too much to worry about propriety. He ached to hold her, to comfort her now that he had discovered the heartache she had hidden from him but he held back. There was much to be said between them before she would feel comfortable with his return.

'No you were very young and trusting. There's nothing to be ashamed about.'

'I think there is in my case,' she whispered. 'You don't know the worst things about me.'

'I saw you both at the graveyard,' admitted Rourke. 'Your maid told me you'd gone riding up there but she didn't tell me you had a companion. I'm ashamed to say that I hid in the trees and watched you. When you and Fisher rode back, I went and had a look to see what took your attention. I understand now why you rejected me and why you were so frightened. It all made sense as soon as I saw that tiny headstone.'

Merry put her head in her hands unable to look at him and felt tears welling up until her shoulders heaved with sobs and the grief stirred up by Jack's visit finally caught up with her. All the loneliness, all the abuse heaped on her by her father and all the struggles she'd endured to keep the farm afloat, especially over the past months, overwhelmed her. She felt Rourke move and sit beside her and his arms held her tightly as she cried.

'Share it with me darling. I'm here for you and I'm not going away. I've come to stay if you'll have me. I don't care about your past. I just want us have a future together.'

Gradually she recovered and gladly took the handkerchief he offered, to wipe her eyes. Taking a deep breath she lifted her head, put her arms around his neck and rested her face against his shoulder. Rourke groaned and pulled her closer kissing her mouth gently and catching a few remaining teardrops with his tongue. He pulled her onto his lap and rocked her gently like a small child until her breathing settled and she calmed down.

'This isn't much of a welcome for you is it?' She managed to say. 'But then I never imagined you would return. And you never wrote to me.'

'Well let's just say when I arrived down in Wellington I felt so wretched at leaving you, I changed my mind. Tobacco farming in Nelson lost its appeal so I cancelled those plans. I went to England instead. Seemed to be a few loose ends there that I needed to tidy up before I really decided where my future lay. I did write but I never posted the letters because I was moving about so much and I failed miserably at expressing how I felt about you. However...' and he reached inside his jacket and pulled out a bundle of envelopes. 'You can read them at your leisure now.'

Merry took them and laughed before she put them on the table. Much as she longed to read them her interest was aroused and she ran her finger down his cheek and across his lips. The letters could wait.

'Don't tell me you went to find the infamous Mrs Findlay?'

'So you remembered?' Rourke kissed her fingertips as they strayed across his mouth.' Yes I did and, what's more I found her.'

'Do tell,' smiled Merry appearing a lot happier and snuggling against him in a way that made him want to carry her off to the nearest bed. He gritted his teeth decided that he must wait until he had told her about his year away.

'It turned out that she wasn't my father's mistress after all but his half sister. Illegitimate of course, and thirty years younger than my father. It seems my grandfather had a renewed lease on life after his son left for America and took a mistress whom he adored. When he died he left mother and child financially sound. My sister, Amelia is her name, knew she had an older brother but nothing else about him. The extraordinary thing is that when her mother died, she became a governess to a young widower with two small daughters and eventually married him. They own a chain of tobacconist shops.'

'Well,' agreed Merry. 'How very strange. That has to be more than a coincidence.'

'Apparently they were looking through some sort of retail news sheet one day and there was an article about my father and his tobacco farm. She recognized his name and wrote to him. Not a begging letter or anything like that according to her but simply introducing herself. It seems my father was so shocked that his father hadn't told him about her that he travelled over to meet her in Brighton. The part where this impacts on us is that he decided to give her the £10,000 that your father owed him. He felt it was due to her as a legacy from their father. She told me she tried to refuse it but he wouldn't have it any other way and eventually the money arrived and she was about to write to thank him only to find out that he'd died. If she had posted the letter none of this would have eventuated.'

'She must've been astonished when you turned up,' said Merry.

'Yes she's my auntie but we're the same age more or less so she felt more like a sister to me. It was a very pleasant reunion and I was able to give her more family background. I ended up spending several weeks in Brighton and London and it gave me time to think about things that were really important to me.'

'And what did you decide?'

'I went back to West Virginia. My brother-in-law had been managing the farm for me in my absence. He and my sister have three children and I felt they needed something of their own so I sold the farm to him. Then I went to San Francisco.'

'And did you visit the Opera?'

Rourke was glad that Merry had not lost her sense of humour and he laughed and shook his head.

'I had some business to attend to then I came home.'

'But I thought you just said you sold your home?'

'As the saying goes "home is where the heart is" and here with you is where my heart is.'

There was no disguising his sincerity and Merry wondered why she had ever doubted him. Was there a future together? Could she offer him her heart and her body without reservation? Gone was the arrogant and cold man who had marched into her house a year ago demanding reparation for her father's debts. In his place a strong warm hearted man who accepted her past and did not judge her. Did she want to continue the lonely life she had led for so long? Or should she grasp the opportunity to go forward with someone who was gazing at her with adoration in those dark, dark eyes?

'You want to stay with a woman who wanted revenge?' She bowed her head. 'I've bitterly regretted not being able to explain my situation to you. Now is the time. Just before my father died he said to me how proud he was I would carry on with the farm. He said it was a great inheritance for me, a dowry if you please. But in reality it was a millstone round my neck. He was so proud because in his sick mind he'd paid off all his debts but to do that he borrowed and left me with a mortgage it will take thirty years to pay off. Well I suppose it's only twenty eight now,' she said considering the maths. 'How delightful to be debt free when I'm fifty five years old and the house has fallen down around me because I've never been able to afford the repairs. How delightful to be still working so hard in all weathers because I cannot afford the staff. Yes I did want revenge but it was on my father Rourke, it should not have been wreaked on you.'

'As things have transpired I can't blame you. My own father was no paragon of virtue before he married. Perhaps if you had revealed everything to me at the beginning we may have reached a better understanding sooner but why would you have told me your secrets? If our circumstances had been reversed I would have acted similarly.'

'I was terrified you would be able to take the

farm from me if I couldn't prove the loan hadn't been repaid. Knowing that the mortgage was my only defence against your demands gave me my only weapon.'

'Well now you don't have to worry about that anymore,' he said. "Or did you already know I paid it?'

Merry swallowed hard and finally looked at him with wide eyes.

'The bank refused to tell me where the money came from and a part of me hoped that it wasn't a terrible book keeping error. But it never occurred to me it was from you.'

'It's my gift to you and I've ensured that this farm will always be in your name whatever happens. However the farm next door now belongs to both of us. I decided we needed a few more acres and the owner was keen to sell.'

Merry looked at him surprised.

'In the last few days I've arranged a special license, a wedding, and a wedding breakfast. I've bought myself a decent horse and last but not least I want to give you this.'

He reached into his jacket pocket and pulled out a small velvet box He handed it to Merry and watched as her fingers trembling, she opened it and revealed a ring with a centre stone of turquoise surrounded by diamonds.

'I love you with all my being. Will you marry me Merryweather Sinclair?'

Rourke got down on his knees in front of her and taking the ring he slid it onto her engagement finger, raised it to his lips and kissed it.

'I don't own a suitable dress,' was the first thing she said practical to the last. She took a deep breath to try and slow down her fast beating heart. 'But apart from that extremely vital fact, yes I do want to marry you and before you say anything else I love you and I do want to have your baby despite everything I said to you before you left. I never wish to be so lonely again as I've been since you left.'

Rourke sat beside her and gave her the gentlest of kisses before he leaned away from her and smiled down at her, his eyes filled love.

'I believe Jane Wyndham and her maid will be calling on you first thing in the morning regarding the dress. It was on my list!'

They both burst out laughing this and Merry threw her arms round his neck and kissed him back with all the ardour he had dreamed of over the past year.

'We do have such a lot to learn about each other,' she said breathless and glowing from his attention. 'But I think that will be great fun and I'm willing to take the risk if you are. In fact I think we should proceed promptly with it. Let me show you my bedroom.'

'Oh sugar,' he whispered in her ear in his best southern drawl as he picked her up and carried her out of the room. 'Little darling, I'm going to have so much fun exploring you.  Can we start now?'

*CHAPTER 18*

In a matter of three days everything had been organized. Merryweather Sinclair entered St John's Church and walked up the aisle on the arm of Gareth Wyndham. She wore a cream silk dress with hand fashioned roses around the neckline and the hem. Fresh roses nestled in her hair and formed her bouquet and when she reached Rourke standing at the altar waiting for her he thought he had never seen any woman so beautiful, so desirable and so confident as the future Mrs Keston.

Their wedding breakfast was held at the Feilding hotel where Rourke was staying and the champagne flowed freely, witty speeches were made and the cake was cut. The happy couple were given a loud send off in Merry's dog cart which had been decorated with white ribbons and flowers. As they set off at a brisk trot up Kimbolton Road, Mary glanced at her husband.

'Where are we going to?'

'Turn round,' ordered Rourke. 'Tell me when you can't see anyone left outside the hotel waving to us.'

Merry did as instructed and as soon as she could see their guests had all disappeared back into the hotel she advised her new husband. Rourke guided the gig around the next left hand corner then the next one again until they were at the back of the hotel they had just set off from. The stable boy came running out, took the horse and Rourke lifted his bride down and guided her into the back entrance, through the kitchen and up the servant stairs, returning to the room where she had dressed earlier in the day. Now it had been transformed, the curtains drawn and lamps giving a soft light. In her absence it had been decorated to turn it into a honeymoon suite with flowers and champagne in a silver ice bucket.

'Well Mrs Keston?'

'What a grand idea Mr Keston,' responded his bride as he found the pins in her hair and started to remove the flowers. 'So practical not to exhaust ourselves on a long trip to somewhere exciting for a honeymoon in exotic places,' she laughed as he unbuttoned her gown and let it drop to the floor revealing her complete nakedness apart from her white silk stockings.

'So practical of you not to waste my time in having to divest you of endless underclothes,' he said as she helped him to remove his wedding suit. 'I wonder I didn't think of it myself.'

But when she unfastened his trousers she found he had nothing underneath either so it was but a very short step to the bed and the sheer joy of lying naked against each other at last as man and wife. Merry held up her hand and admired the beautiful hand beaten rose gold wedding ring her husband had placed on her finger at their wedding ceremony.

'I forgot to thank you for this,' she whispered as his fingers caressed her and his mouth lingered on her breasts. He lifted his head and gave her a wink.

'That was why I had to return to San Francisco. It wasn't to attend the opera but to collect up some gold and have it made for you. I wanted you to have something unique, something no-one else has ever received from me because I've never met another woman like you.'

He returned to his exploration of her body but felt her stiffen beneath him.

'What do you mean you collected some gold,' she said slowly. 'Did you go into the hills with a hammer and a bucket and just by chance find a seam of gold?'

The suspicion in her voice sent a slight shiver of pleasure through his body and he chose his next words very carefully, very carefully indeed. His new wife had pride in herself and her hard work and he had not been entirely honest with her about his circumstances.

'Well I own a gold mine…or maybe two or three and then there's a silver mine somewhere…'

Merry grabbed his head and forced him to look at her.

'You own gold mines? You told me you were a simple tobacco farmer! You lying toad! Did you ever need that money?'

He tried to hang his head in mock shame but his relief in finally being able to share his good fortune with her forced him to sit up and confess.

'As I told you before it was a matter of honour I believed I owed something to my father mistaken or not, but no I didn't need it. I should have told you but I knew you would think I was offering you charity if I gave in too easily.'

Merry squinted up at him and then stretched her arms above her head against the satin pillows in such a wanton pose he had to look away before he silenced her with a ravenous kiss.

'So...'' she said slowly. 'I should have guessed when I noticed your cufflinks. Real nuggets eh? Not some cheap imitation?'

'Mmm...Yep,' he admitted. 'I had them made from my first lucky strike. I was still arrogant then.'

'Oh...' she sighed and stroked her fingers over his stomach. 'So you're not arrogant any longer?'

'I like to think I changed when I met you darling.'

'It's just that...' she sighed again and pointed down at his obvious and very virile erection. 'That looks pretty arrogant to me!'

'Indeed it does,' he also sighed. 'I must have forgotten to instruct it.'

'Thank God,' said his wife and pulled him down as she lifted her legs around his waist and dealt very proficiently and capably with said arrogance until they both begged for mercy from each other in the most wonderful and loving way.

## *EPILOGUE*

It was six months since they had departed on a prolonged honeymoon and Mr and Mrs Keston were both very pleased to be coming home and to see the gates of Greenleigh appear. As Rourke guided the dog cart up the driveway he heard the gasp his wife gave as the house came into sight.

'It's been painted!'

Her husband looked down at her and grinned at her excitement. He was growing used to her enthusiasm that had been re-kindled since their marriage. Now she was his wife he had been able to take care of all the problems and loneliness that had dogged her for so many years. In turn she had removed all his brooding thoughts and pent up emotions with her unending affectionate touches and glances. She had simply not allowed him to exert his old arrogant attitudes into their life together, always teasing, always sharing her earthy humour with him until he had to laugh and chase her and love her.

She had agreed to his hiring a reputable farm manager and more staff while they travelled to America to meet his family. To add to the pleasure his English aunt Amelia and her husband and children had come to stay in West Virginia for a huge family gathering that might have overwhelmed Merry. But she embraced them all with the hunger of someone who endured years without family or affection. Her mother-in-law was delighted to welcome her and already there were plans for her to visit New Zealand and stay with her son and wife.

Merry drew in a deep breath as they stopped outside the house and even before she could alight from the cart, the door opened and her maid, and a whole legion of staff trooped out to welcome them. Inside the hallway the wood panelling had been re varnished and fresh flowers filled the air with the scent of spring.

Tea was ordered and Rourke helped his wife take off her coat. They entered the drawing room where all the furniture had been re-furbished, new curtains hung and soft duck egg blue wallpaper replaced the faded brown pattern.

'It was Jane's idea,' said Rourke watching his wife spin round as she took in the new splendour of the room. 'I said she could do this room, the dining room and our bedroom but to leave everything else to you when we got back. Oh! Something else too — a new bathroom with running water.'

'It's wonderful. I love it,' said Merry. 'I can never thank you enough Rourke. You anticipate my every wish. I do know exactly which room I'll renovate next.'

'A bedroom for my mother?' said her husband hopefully.

'Ah yes that will certainly be second on the list.'

She was up to something Rourke guessed by the mischievous smile she gave him as she came close and put her arms around him. He cleared his throat as she took his face in her hands and gave him a deep welcome home sort of kiss that filled him with heat and longing. Then she drew back and put her head on one side.

'Can't you guess?' she teased.

Rourke tensed as he began to understand those long private conversations between his mother, sister and Merry.

'You mean the reason my Mama is coming all this way is…?'

'We're having a baby my darling.'

Rourke was filled with joy and concern all at the same moment.

'Are you well? I thought women were always sick? You've been no different than your usual self.'

'I must be one of the lucky ones I think. I wasn't sick with Alexander and not with this one either.'

'I shall order the best doctor for you, midwives, day and night nurses, wet nurses, sweetheart. I promise nothing will go wrong this time.'

His anxiety made her smile a little sadly and she nestled against him with a reassurance he could feel as she held him tightly.

'I'm sure it won't but if it does I'll have your support this time and I can't ask for anything more than that.'

'We'll call him Storm and Sky if it's a girl,' chuckled Rourke knowing she would not agree.

'I was thinking more 'Hale and Shine', she said with a cheeky look up at him.

'For better or worse,' whispered Rourke resigned to her humour. 'I'd better start designing a nursery. Do you think I could buy a train set?'

'I'm sure she'll love that but don't forget the dolls for him!'

If you enjoyed reading *Sweet Bitter Revenge,* you may like to read the love story of Gareth and Jane Wyndham.

*Sweet Bitter Waters* reveals their past secrets and how after murder, kidnapping and cruelty they achieve what seems impossible when they first meet, a deep and everlasting love born of courage and endurance.

*Sweet Bitter Waters* is a Rangitawa Romance by Carole St Aubyns, set in rural New Zealand in 1888. 16+


*Vote for Love* by Jemma Daintree is set against the background of New Zealand women fighting for the vote. Rural school teacher Lydia Langford is seduced by her local politician and then sent to the capital Wellington to help present the petition for electoral reform. She enters into a loveless marriage and becomes a member of the notorious Aphrodite Club where women pay be pleasured by men skilled in physical arts. Will she find true love again? *Vote for love* explores an era when women were becoming more liberated and seeking their own right to enjoy passion. The first book in the Aphrodite Club series. 18+